NEAR MORTAL

Julia Alty

Story Quarry

Story
Quarry

ISBN-13: 978-1-7375657-0-3

Editorial guidance provided by: Mackenzie Winder of InkCorrigible Edits.

Cover design by: Julia Alty

Library of Congress Control Number: 2021914008

Printed in the United States of America
City of publication Glendale, Arizona

Visit www.altyart.com for permission to use passages from Near Mortal.

While there have been so many people that have helped arrive at the end of this first novel, this dedication truly belongs to:

Carol Ann Kreutz.

Who always believed in my creative endeavors and inspired me to never give up.

NEAR MORTAL

1

Orange.

Pink.

Plumes of white.

Each color mingles together in the expansive, cloud-covered sky. Light pinks give way to vibrant oranges, causing a Creamsicle-like vista. The scene pulls *Oohs* and *Aahs* from Peter's fellow travelers in the dining car. Taking a quick break from the chapter he's creating, Peter rubs his sore neck and quickly glances out the window at what he would call a decent sunset. Satisfied with this glimpse, he returns to his leather-bound notebook. Planted on a solid wood stool in this slow-moving Steamline, he's already been writing and sketching fervently into his notebook for hours, enough material inside of him from his recent travels to continue writing for days.

Peter continues to write as the sunset concludes and most of the passengers depart. Observing such beauty typically inspires him, but when struck by his inner sense of creativity his surroundings always fall to the wayside, leaving him to ardently forge his tome one moment at a time. It's a world history from his perspective, constructed not only with the written word but with drawings and the occasional archeological artifact pressed into the pages to add a tactile element. From ticket stubs to dried-out flora, they add more texture to his timeline collage.

Some may call what he's made beautiful and creative. *Art*, even. But to Peter the title *historian* rings much truer than artist. Coming from a line of great entertainers, Peter was born with the need to create, yet not the yearning to share. In his younger years he'd given acting a try, and while he was decent—starring in a few indie films that gained notoriety—it never truly fulfilled him.

Turning his attention to the written word, he worked towards publishing some of his drawings and observations. His writing conjured up scenes from his youth, an era long lost and nearly forgotten. But even with a library full of his published works and raving reviews, Peter found that only the physical act of *creating* fulfilled him. Having lost any interest in pursuing a way for others to see his work, Peter continues to construct his volumes but now keeps them to himself.

With a few sleepy blinks, the cabin lights kick on and the last bit of natural light gives way to the impending darkness. This snaps Peter out of his reminiscing and back to the exterior world. Unable to return to his writings, he rubs his day-old scruff, sets his pen down, and closes his journal. He massages the back of his neck a little as he scans the dining car, looking for his next piece of inspiration.

And inspiration he finds.

Crossing the threshold into the dining car and clutching a small vinyl suitcase with both hands is the most alluring woman he's ever seen.

She must have just recently boarded, he thinks as he places his pen in his shirt pocket. Peter suddenly becomes very self-conscious of his appearance as he runs his hands down the front of his shirt, his fingers searching out any wrinkles and smoothing them as well as he can. Glancing at his reflection in the window, Peter runs his hands through his short dark hair a few times, more out of nerves than vanity.

Drawn immediately to this stranger, Peter takes his notebook in hand and makes his way to the bar at the front of the dining car. Not wanting to be too obvious in his approach, Peter barely throws a glance in her direction, taking her in just long enough to notice her long cascades of wavy mocha hair gently swaying with the jostling of the train. Leaning up against the countertop, Peter throws a smile her way and deliberately clears his throat, hoping to gain her attention naturally and to not have to figure out how to advance. This, to no one's surprise, does not work. Peter watches as she finishes her order, handing over the cash due in exact change before walking off to one of the booths, never once glancing his way.

Peter watches as she walks away, racking his brain to put a finger on what exactly draws him to this woman. Romanticism had been purged from his character centuries ago, so there is no *love at first sight* ideology at play. While she is attractive, she is not astoundingly so. No other men are currently fawning at her feet. Yet there is something about the way she holds herself, as if she is presenting herself to the world instead of just being in it. There's a magnetic force that she exudes that draws him in even now as she takes a seat in the dining car.

"What can I get yah?" the server asks Peter, who is still leaning against the counter trying to be casual with his gaze.

Absorbed in watching this woman, Peter had momentarily forgotten that he's standing next to a bar, and that the purpose of such is to order food and drink. The server's question causes Peter to let out a small and barely noticeable yelp accompanied by a slight jump. He turns back to see the bartender watching him with amusement.

"Oh, um. Nothing right now, thank you," Peter replies, giving the counter a tap before he walks away, trying to look as nonchalant as possible. Peter finds that the yellow tint of the lights in the dining car creates a warm and inviting feeling, making it even more appealing to continue with his quest to meet this woman.

"Pull it together, man!" Peter chides under his breath as he makes his way towards her seat, tripping over his own feet in the process. Fortunately, the booth seats are all facing away with their backs to the front of the car, so Peter can approach without the woman seeing his sudden bout of clumsiness. Spying an open seat directly across from her, he continues his stumble down the aisle. While usually exceptionally good at picking up ladies, the idea that there's something special about this woman has worked its way into his head, creating the complete buffoon that is his current condition.

At least luck is on my side, he thinks as he nears the open seat, fully intent on saying something very clever to her on his descent. But what he plans to say slips away from him with every step he takes closer. So much so that by the time he arrives directly behind her row he can barely remember his own name, let alone a come-on that is worthy of such a beauty.

But as he was thinking before being interrupted by the barkeep, it really isn't just her looks that draw him to her. From the striking green eyes that he could see the moment she first entered the dining car to the elegant blue dress that truly sets them off and complements every aspect of her body, Peter finds himself lost in the allure of this individual. This woman.

His inability to find words makes him momentarily consider turning around and going back to his sleeping car. He could try again later. But he knows he can't give up.

I've come this far, he thinks to himself. *The least I can do is sit.*

So sit he does.

2

The boarding pass she's been provided works perfectly and Mandy finds herself filled with a childlike excitement as she climbs the three steps onto the train, resisting the urge to skip down the long hallway with pure joy. Being raised near train tracks like these but never having been rich enough to ride the rails, she had always longed for the day she would be a passenger and not merely an observer.

Continuing down the aisle, she thinks to herself, *That day is today.*

However, Mandy's excitement quickly turns on her as impostor syndrome kicks in, making her feel like a fraud. Even alone in the hallway, she has a feeling that someone at any moment will point her out as they did at the end of the original *Body Snatchers* film; raising one hand, an index finger stretched out straight at her, and releasing a noise that is in no way human to alert all to her presence.

This image shakes loose as the train jolts forward and she braces herself against one of the hallway walls. Catching herself in these spiraling negative thoughts, she can fortunately correct herself. While she may not have been the one to purchase the train ticket, she knows she belongs here. And more importantly, she has a job to do.

Straightening up her posture a little, Mandy continues walking down the narrow hallway and muses to herself that even as the world has quickly changed around her, she is happy that trains like this one have stood the test of time. She glances to her left, catching her reflection in the darkening windows that line the aisle. Pausing for a moment, she takes note that she truly looks like she belongs in this upper-class setting.

Standing among the privileged and doing a damn good job looking like I belong, she assures herself. Mandy then shakes off any last bit of doubt and feels the train pick up its last bit of speed. Clutching the small case she has with both hands, she enters the dining car.

Stepping through the entrance, she's crestfallen. The interior of the car is much smaller than she'd imagined in her youth. Her hunger, however, distracts her from any childhood disappointment she may feel as she heads straight to the bar. Her mission falls momentarily to the wayside as she reads over the menu. While enjoying the diverse options, she also finds the incredibly clean plastic covering of the menu useful to catch the reflection of the man that would soon be of her affection. Observing that he's already watching her, a smile graces her face, paired with the realization that she's slightly ahead of the game and can now focus on this delicious menu.

After a few moments, Mandy chooses an assorted fruit and cheese plate. The bartender, a slim man in his early twenties, takes her order down on a screen and then asks for her fingerprint for payment.

"Oh no, I have this," Mandy says as she removes a change purse from a side pocket in her dress, paying him with cash. The bartender takes a pause, sighs at the unconventional payment method, and takes the bills, working out the change due on his fingers.

Mandy can now feel the presence of her target at the bar and hears a slight, not-so-subtle clearing of his throat. Wanting to make her conquest a little more challenging and curious about all the *ladies' man* stories she's heard about this gentleman, she quickly thanks the bartender, grabs her change, and moves deeper into the dining car.

With the train nearly at capacity, Mandy initially finds it hard to locate the right seat. Needing to maintain her confidence, she continues walking down the narrow aisle. For a brief moment she considers turning back and simply chatting her target up at the bar, seeing as he's already in pursuit of her. Disheartened by the idea, Mandy pauses for a moment and is rewarded by a woman rising from her aisle seat and exiting the dining car. Figuring she can easily take care of her seatmate, Mandy immediately takes this seat and turns to the gentlemen occupying the seat across the aisle.

"I'll give you a twenty to go anywhere else," she states, discreetly flashing a bill between her fingers. Without a word, the man reaches out his hand, accepts the twenty, and heads straight off.

Didn't want to make it too hard, she thinks to herself as she settles into her seat and pulls her tray down. Seeing the server coming up the aisle with her food, she's impressed by the speed of delivery and relieved that she'll have a couple moments to eat something before her big conquest.

Closing her eyes to savor this moment, Mandy pops a gorgeous green olive into her mouth and follows it immediately with a surprisingly sweet, almost caramelly cheese. Savoring the mix of flavors, she continues this routine a few more times until she senses her target approaching once more. Mandy continues to eat—now choosing a pear slice with some brie followed by a swirl of honey accompanied by a chunk of blue cheese—constantly running scenarios through her head the entire time, working out the best way to approach as he takes the bait and sits down in the seat across from her.

Fortunately, her food decides for her. One green olive in particular. She takes it between her thumb and forefinger and raises it towards her mouth, but having plans of its own, the olive leaps out of her grasp and across the aisle into the lap of the man she is intent on meeting. Looking the other way, he seems oblivious to this development.

After a moment of staring at him, the bright green circle now securely in his lap, Mandy leans nearer to him across the aisle.

3

There Peter sits, staring out the window, working out how to talk to a pretty girl.

Hi had always worked when he was younger, but the girls were younger then too. Even though his outward appearance stopped aging around his midthirties, he no longer has any interest in women that *Hi* works on.

A smile skims across his face as he thinks back on some of them, his memories flashing before him like a flipbook. He reflects first on his longer relationships, the few there'd been. They were the ones that made him feel alive. Alive, but distant, as he learned early on that he cannot stand the idea of outliving someone he deeply loves. This realization led to a change in his dating habits, where he instead found a new woman every week for years. More years than he wants to admit.

Absorbed in this train of thought, Peter fails to notice that mere moments after he's sat down the woman he is drawn to has focused in on him and is currently working on attaining his attention. He only notices when out of nowhere—at least from his perspective—there comes a dainty, "Hi?"

Peter nearly yelps again as he quickly swivels his head towards the *Hi* and finds the gorgeous woman's face to be nearly touching his own. Unable to see beyond her astounding emerald eyes, the kind that would make him weak in the knees had he been standing, Peter feels both a magnetic pull to her and immobilization at the same time. When he's finally able to shake himself free of her gaze, Peter squeezes out a weak *Hi* of his own.

"This is pretty embarrassing," Mandy whispers, inching even closer to him.

"Yes?" Peter manages to get out, leaning in a bit himself.

"You seem to have one of my olives," she continues with a slight smirk on her face as she motions to his lap.

"Oh?" Peter responds coyly, taking a second for what she said to sink in. He follows her gesture and finds, sure enough, there is a tiny green ball in his lap. "Oh!" he repeats with a slight chuckle and hands over the olive, their fingertips briefly touching.

"Thanks," she responds with a smile, quickly turning to her tray to return the olive to its cohorts before looking back at Peter, who is still halfway in the aisle.

The ice is broken, Peter thinks to himself, and it is now his turn to talk. He knows this. He is ready. He opens his mouth, but before he can utter a single syllable he's interrupted by her seatmate shuffling to exit the booth. She quickly gets up to allow the seatmate to pass, standing so close to Peter that her dress brushes up against his cheek. The soft, cool silk reminds him of a rose petal. Mandy coyly turns her head just enough to look down over her shoulder at Peter.

"Would you care to join me? Might be easier than leaning into the aisle," she offers.

Without a word or hesitation, Peter leaps over and past Mandy, landing in the window seat. With a slight smirk, Mandy retakes her seat and picks a little at the remainder of her cheese plate. She motions towards the plate as an offer to Peter, but he declines. He's still trying to conjure up something more than a monosyllabic response. Just as the silence is beginning to stretch out too long, Peter finally settles on the first and only thing he can think of. As cliché as it is, he needs to loosen his tongue.

"So, do you take this line often?" he asks as smoothly as possible while Mandy finishes a bite of cheese.

"Oh no," Mandy replies, wiping remnants of cheese off her fingers and pushing the plate as close to the aisle as possible. "This is my first Steamline voyage. You?"

"I do most of my travel by Steamline. I hate all forms of air travel and love seeing the countryside. I find it very inspiring,"

Peter responds, feeling more like himself with every word.

"Inspiring?" she inquires as she leans in a little closer to him. "Personally? Or are you an artist, perchance?"

"Not really an artist," he says and reciprocates her movement. "I've tried the artist route a few times, but most of my creations tend to be more for personal pleasure than any kind of exhibition."

"What is it you do then?" she asks, remaining close.

"That's hard to sum up, but you could say that I'm in sales," he answers, not ready to give away too much information about his past, or that he basically peddles comic books for a living. He attempts to read her face but is unable to gauge her actual interest.

"Sales," Mandy echoes, trying not to show her surprise in realizing she really knows excruciatingly little about her target. She takes solace in the fact that her naivety will be to her advantage, as it will translate as genuine interest in getting to know him.

"Right," Peter responds, finally feeling in complete control of himself. "One could say," he continues as he reaches past her to the platter of food and pops an olive into his mouth, "I'm in possession of certain goods that others pay quite a bit to own themselves." Peter leans back into his seat but makes sure to keep as close to her as possible.

"Well, that all sounds quite..." she begins, pausing for dramatic effect. "Mysterious," Mandy finishes as she scoots a little closer, being near enough that their noses almost touch.

"That's kinda the point," he counters with a sly grin that sends an electric charge through Mandy. Both remain in this space, so close they would barely need to move to kiss, feeling the electricity of the moment flowing between them.

"Miss?" comes a timid voice beside Mandy. "I'm sorry, but the kitchen is closing. Are you done with this?"

Letting out a lengthy sigh, Mandy turns to look at the young woman, who is slightly red in the face from interrupting. Embarrassed for the server, Mandy nods that the plate is ready to go and slips her a hearty tip in appreciation. She then turns back to Peter, who during this interaction has sat back deep in his seat.

Knowing he's been following her since the moment she stepped foot into the dining car and tired of waiting for his *ladies' man* persona to appear, Mandy internally takes a deep breath and externally puts on a face of confidence, raising an eyebrow as she turns back to Peter.

"You wanna get out of here?"

"Absolutely!" he replies, nearly cutting off the end of her question and immediately regretting the speed in which his words escape. Not noticing the swift response and relieved that her bravery is paying off, Mandy gracefully grabs the case in her left hand and him in her right.

"After you," she whispers as she motions for him to lead the way.

Peter gladly takes the lead as they continue holding hands down the hallway. Mandy trails ever so slightly behind him, occasionally bumping into Peter's back as the train rocks from side to side. The pair are giggling like children by the time they arrive at the door, which Peter quickly unlocks, and they explode into the room. Wanting to keep the momentum going, Mandy does the first thing she can think of and begins to undress.

"I didn't catch your name," Mandy says as she unbuttons the front of her dress. After fumbling with the lock on the door, Peter turns around.

"Peter," he answers and pauses for a follow-up question, wanting to keep up with the speed of his companion's clothing removal. Pulling his button-up shirt off over his head, he manages to inquire about her name as her dress falls to the ground, revealing an attractive array of undergarments.

"Peter, huh?" she coos, taking a moment to watch as he stumbles over his pant legs on his way towards the couch. "Then I must be the wolf," she finishes as she crosses to Peter, who's now sitting on the couch.

The *Peter and the Wolf* reference throws Peter off for a

moment, knowing—as is his job—that there have been no copies of *Peter and the Wolf* in circulation for over a century, minus the few housed in museums. With Peter lost in a whirlwind of questions about this woman, it is Mandy who delivers the first kiss.

Enjoying her role as seductress, she gently kisses him while lowering her body onto his lap. Peter returns the kiss, causing Mandy to pull back a little with a teasing smile, still wanting to maintain some control. She leans back in only to suspend her lips near enough that it creates a light caress but not any kind of true pressure, keeping the tension building for as long as she can stand. Feeling his breathing pattern speed up, she now knows two things: that this will be one of her top five lifetime kisses and that both of them are ready for a long night together. Letting go, Mandy finally connects with Peter's lips as they press into each other with a passion neither have ever experienced. They relish in the immediate and delicious taste of each other, proving to each the beautiful compatibility of their bodies.

Emboldened by this kiss, in one fluid movement Peter reclines the couch into a bed and swings Mandy around onto her back. A look of surprise crosses her face for a moment, but she adjusts quickly to the change of speed and can now see the man described to her. As he slowly moves his way down her body, she can't help but derive pleasure out of not only the intense sensations shooting through her but also from her knowledge that he is *her* conquest.

4

Peter stirs at the lurch of the train gaining momentum after the first stop of the morning. Taking a deep breath as he rolls over on his back, he catches the scent of his companion. He involuntarily reaches across the bed for her only to find her side cool and empty. He had hoped that her line about departing from the train early had been just that—a line. He sits up and stretches out the kinks in his back from sleeping on a converted sofa bed, twisting left to right and back again. Last night is still running through his head as he glances at the clock on the nightstand and sees that there is plenty of time before his own departure.

Lying back down, Peter runs through both the physical escapades and the equally stimulating pillow talk from the previous night. He had revealed more about himself than he had in over a decade. It dawns on him that he'd done most of the talking and now gleefully floats with the light feeling that only comes from being truly heard.

Dying to tell someone about his amazing night, he taps the communication device on his right temple, about to connect to his best friend and business partner when he receives an alert that he has an incoming call. Tapping once on his temple, he is told by a pleasant robotic woman's voice that the incoming call is from none other than Jonah.

"Jonah! I was just about to ring you," Peter states, beginning the process of packing up his things.

"Well, a happy coincidence indeed. But before you go into one of your *Hi Girl* stories—"

"*Hi Girls*? Is that what you call them?"

"Yes, and you really are getting too old for that by the way.

Like a century too old, but that's not why I called. I need to—"

"No, wait," Peter interrupts as he sits down on the edge of his unmade bed. "Just because I was going to call you does not mean I was calling because of a girl."

There is a pause and a sigh as Jonah realizes Peter's thing must come first.

"Alright, fair enough. What's up?"

"Thank you," Peter says as he stands up and paces. "Anyway, as I was saying, I met the most amazing *woman* last night."

"Peter! Come on!" Jonah groans, not hiding his frustration.

"Not a *Hi Girl* as you call them, but an actual blow-me-out-of-the-water *woman*. Although now that I think about it, our conversation began with her saying 'hi'... But that's beyond the point," Peter explains, pausing just long enough for Jonah to jump in.

"That's all well and good," Jonah interjects. "But seriously, I called for a reason. I need to confirm all of your drops today. The second one in particular has been very antsy about getting their goods."

"Yes, yes," Peter relents as he stops pacing and resumes his packing routine. "I'm on route now. I will be right on schedule, assuming the first drop doesn't delay me."

"Just this once, Peter, please make sure it doesn't. With one drop you will be able to fund yourself, and me, for the next three years." The sound of typing bleeds through on Jonah's end as he finishes his sentence. Peter rolls his eyes, having already heard about the importance of this patron numerous times.

"Yes, Jonah, I know. Now about this woman—"

"Sorry, Pete, I've got a lot of calls to return today. Even with this big fish you're landing, it's a buyer's market out here. And if I don't get the leads, your lures will stop... Okay, I lost the metaphor, but you get where I'm going, and go I must." Peter hears Jonah's typing speed up and can tell this isn't the time to recount his experience.

"You're an idiot, but I get it. No time for my tale now. Fine. Just know you're in for an amazing story later," Peter quips, trying to hide his disappointment.

"I'll be sure to have a fresh bottle of wine ready in anticipation," Jonah replies in a distant tone.

"Fresh bottle? Funny," Peter comes back.

"I try," Jonah finishes and disconnects, leaving Peter to finish packing.

Always traveling light, Peter's done packing within ten minutes and is off to the dining car for a quick breakfast. His favorite stool next to the largest window is open, and after he places his order Peter settles in, staring out the window at the now very urban landscape. He takes in the inordinately tall buildings that take up the majority of space within the downtown area of The City. Despite the suburban areas being laid out in a grid-like fashion, the urban sprawl of downtown is more like a weed garden, with skyscrapers seemingly battling each other to reach the limits of the troposphere.

Thoughts of the day ahead of him, the chaos of taking an Air Cab, and the happy but demanding clients cloud his head. Peter turns his attention back to the interior of the dining car just in time to be greeted by his simple breakfast of a blueberry scone and coffee. Taking a sip, he finds that all thoughts of his pending day slowly fade away to *her*.

The Wolf.

5

It may not have been in The Director's plans, but the moment Mandy accepted her assignment she knew exactly where she'd depart from the train. The perfect place for her to gather whatever thoughts she'd be grappling with after her seduction by—or in this turn of events, seduction *of*—the *infamous Peter*. She would head straight to her safe space, a secluded spot she'd turned to many times in her life when the need to reflect and think arose. A place that happens to have a perfect view of the local train station, giving Mandy the ability to take a quick detour before returning to the afternoon Steamline that has a direct route into the heart of The City. She can stay on schedule and, hopefully, leave The Director none the wiser.

The City itself is mapped out on a grid structure, using all allotted space to its maximum potential. The importance of using every square inch came after The Collision, or what others referred to as the Reverse Pangea Incident. Although she wasn't alive herself during this event, Mandy still remembers well every lesson about it from grade school. How with little warning the continents slammed together with slingshot-like swiftness, creating immense mountain ranges and tsunamis that washed over more than half the land. The anomaly killed off billions of people and left those alive with the task of literally rebuilding the world. No longer separated by massive bodies of water, all cultures had to come together as one.

Human nature being what it is, once the initial shock of this catastrophic event wore off the decades of war began, a direct result of vastly different cultures clashing together. The chaos and bloodshed only halted once the strategy of creating one massive and insulated community came into play. People could then have their own spaces and communities. And despite the tight living quarters, The City's mapped-out separation gave humanity a new sense of unity.

Both scientists and engineers banded together to map out the new continent, keeping wide-open spaces for farming communities in the southern region and designing a sprawling metropolis area for industrial work and living space in the north. Finally, with the help of new technologies developed prior to The Collision initially designed for planetary development, they also created The Air City and all its branch-off colonies. Both communities were designed to house a multitude of people, with the metropolitan area sprawling out more on the ground level and continuously growing vertically in the sky.

As Mandy walks through The City, she marvels over how the ability to live airborne had been the monumental turning point for their civilization. A moment of self-awareness makes her laugh out loud at herself. She's supposed to be sorting through her current dilemma regarding the assignment, not dwelling on a fourth-grade history lesson.

Mandy finds herself passing through this cookie-cutter landscape. Within each ten-block radius there are high-rise housing developments, one school, and a lone grocery store. Then the pattern repeats. High-rises, school, grocery store. The communities had been designed to make the living areas simpler for those that choose the metropolis lifestyle. The infrastructure would work so well that it would then be duplicated as The Air City began to development.

Even with the cookie-cutter layout, or perhaps because of it, each grid exists within smaller subcommunities. Neighborhoods are based on a variety of factors depending on the people that settled in them. In a small way, this division reminds Mandy of her childhood. Growing up in The City herself, she fell in love at a young age with the various cultures she could experience with every move she made throughout her fosterhood. Within these subsections, she found that there would always be a change in atmosphere as she passed from one area to the next. Even the most ordinary of city blocks, one where none of the neighbors interacted, had its own ambience, creating the vast box of crayons that color the landscape that is The City.

Occasionally there would be a blending effect, with one community's identity bleeding over to the next. The best side effect of this, in Mandy's opinion, has to be the creation of the most delicious food you could ever experience. The fusion of cultural delicacies is a perk of living in The City that she used to take advantage of a lot more. However, more often than not she feels as if she's walking over literal boundary lines as she passes from one block to the next.

Heading now to *her spot*, case tight in hand, Mandy can't help but think more about the massive undertaking it must have been to plot out this world they now live in. Even beyond the urban landscape, these brilliant men and women mapped the rest of the continental space down to the last plot of land. From the agricultural fields to the mountainous regions, every available patch of earth has been put to good use.

As she makes her way deeper into the neighborhood, Mandy begins to reflect on her previous visits to this particular hideaway, the one she considers her home away from home. Although she's explored innumerable communities in her childhood, she finds herself gravitating to this one most. She initially fell in love with the acts of kindness and the genuine sense of community that she rarely experienced elsewhere; one person offering to carry another's groceries from the cab to their front door, people holding open doors for one another, and children helping their elders cross the street. These simple gestures made a large impact on a younger Mandy and moved her towards the social justice work she does today.

Aside from the pay-it-forward attitude each individual seems to have here, this block also holds regularly scheduled street parties and fairs. Drawing near her destination, Mandy hears the familiar sound of party music mixed with children's laughter. An electric excitement runs through her body as she picks up her pace. Now only one block away, Mandy notices a few pieces of hay blow past her feet. As she finally rounds the corner, Mandy spots a nearby bale of hay being used as a seat for two teenagers, their fingers intertwined behind their backs and strands of hay letting loose as their fingers play the ravel-unravel game. A smile graces Mandy's face as she makes her way through the crowd, passing several barbeques and tables showcasing a sea of side dishes. The smells, delicious. The sights, glorious. If she didn't have more important things on her mind, Mandy would be tempted to stop and blend in.

At least long enough for a helping of that magnificent cherry pie, she thinks to herself as she instead heads down a side alley. With a single leap, she grabs hold of the fire escape ladder and pulls it down with her momentum. Her small case in hand, Mandy fumbles her way to the top. Here she can rest until the familiar stream of white steam can be seen in the distance from her vista point, signaling to her it's time to make her way back to the Steamline for her original arrival time at The Facility.

Setting her case down near the ladder, she goes to the opposite side of the building where she can take in the sights of the block party below. Mandy watches the children running and laughing, shooting water guns at each other. The shy pair of teens on the haystack steal a kiss before getting a squirt from one of the neighbor kids, prompting the teenage boy to chase after the entire hoard. These moments bring a smile to Mandy's face and allow some of her own childhood memories to resurface. Her mother, a Near Mortal, passed away as she came into the world, and her father died just days later in a car accident. Mandy was raised in the mostly uncaring world of foster homes, knowing the feeling of community only when she was within a neighborhood such as this, where it is brought to you.

Back during her childhood, before the category of Near Mortal had been conceptualized, she'd known she was different but did not understand to what extent until people she loved began to age much faster than she did. Others would make jokes about her skincare and exercise routines, but behind the jokes there was always a curiosity she didn't know how to answer, so she would move on. Her entire adult life ended up being exactly like that of her childhood. She bounced around from one place to another, never feeling like she belonged anywhere until she found refuge in her current career at The Facility.

Sitting down on the rooftop, Mandy leans her back against the siding, hands resting on her belly, taking a moment to enjoy her alone time. A scarce thing these days. Mandy closes her eyes and pictures the end of her mission. With the first phase behind her, uncertainty begins to fill her. Taking a deep breath, she stands back up and sits on the adjacent ledge, having a perfect view of the train's path. Here she can sit and be still until that first hint of white hits the vibrant blue of the sky.

6

Mortal

Near Mortal

Immortal

Overpopulation

New World

The list on Tian's blackboard stands tall in his tiny office, the words *New World* circled with vigor. Even with all the advancements made in technology, chalk is still his preferred method for list making, especially in setting personal goals and focusing in on problems that need his specific attention. Agendas he knows he alone will solve.

That is the point of The Facility after all. To help the world, to change it. As the mission statement says: *To Create A Safe Place For The Entirety Of The Human Race To Thrive.* To learn from the ever-evolving genome. From Tian's perspective, to steer it to the correct course. His course. They created The Facility to help make this change possible. And change is all that is currently on Tian's mind.

Adjusting his levitating chair to kick his feet up on his desk, Tian sits with his hands laced behind his head, staring at the list on the chalkboard and contemplating all the actions already set in motion. Moving his gaze from the chalkboard to the papers on his desk, his more devolved list catches his eye and brings a smile to his face as he sees all the items ceremoniously crossed off. He's right on track, ready to keep his workflow just that—flowing.

Lost in his own glory, Tian jolts up from the buzz of his intercom. Moving towards the device, he kicks his feet off his desk and the chair lowers slightly to allow his feet to connect with the floor. He pushes the brightly flashing button.

"Yes?" he says flatly, finding himself impatient at this interruption.

"Sir, Mandy checked in via text. Her mission is complete. Our agents say that she has taken a detour but seems to be watching for the next train. Assuming she catches this next one, she should be back by her intended check-in time."

Even with Mandy's detour, Tian cannot keep a smile from spreading across his face.

"This is splendid news! I'll be up in a few moments. Thank you."

"You're welcome, sir," the young man's voice says as the line quickly disconnects.

Sitting up straight, Tian takes one more glance at his list on the board before scanning the room for any items he might need before leaving. The news of Mandy's detour is a little concerning, but it's not out of character for her. After spending months training Mandy, it does not surprise him that she'd need some time after this first step. He'd just hoped she would do so on her train ride back to him. But anger wasn't his first, or even fifth emotion, really.

I may not even bring it up during her debriefing, Tian thinks as he closes his door behind him, still maintaining his smile, and both manually and electronically locks it. He leaves the door with his *This Is Not An Exit* sign up to ensure no one tries to enter without his knowledge, then heads to his public office upstairs.

Quickly making his way through the vast warehouse structure his preferred office is located in, he passes floor-to-ceiling shelving units, mostly empty, with aisles too long to see to the ends of. His shoes create a slight echo as he walks past dozens of rows, arriving at an elevator whose doors open immediately at the push of the only button. *Up.* Tian steps inside and gleefully taps the lone button present in the elevator. The doors close, leaving him with a moment of silence as he swiftly moves to the above-ground facility. Sliding open moments later, the elevator deposits him into a closet-sized room with spectacular halogen lighting and a full-length mirror in which he adjusts his tie before exiting.

He closes the door to this secret elevator behind him, revealing a sign on it reading *Janitor Supplies*. Tian walks down a long, skinny hall to the main lobby of the building, ducking in through the bamboo garden that hides its existence. From the lobby, he heads straight down a side hallway to a door with the label *Director*. Opening this door, he has arrived at his public office space.

The polar opposite of his other office, any modern technology is replaced by much older pieces of rundown equipment. Where his blackboard of goals downstairs would hang is a collection of vintage posters quoting self-esteem boosting mottos such as "Some excel because they are destined to. Others excel because they are determined to." Mixed in are a couple newer posters with slogans boasting the importance of working together regardless of race, gender, or life expectancy. Since Tian can't help but cringe each time he sees one, he's had them hung up behind his desk and out of eyesight.

He leaves the door open and sits down at his desk, kicking his feet up once again. Grabbing a tablet, he begins to read the most recent reports sent to him from his field workers. He tries hard to respond quickly, as they all are waiting for his response before moving forward with any work they have. But his concentration wavers as he finds his mind circling back to what Mandy has achieved and how excited he is that at this very moment she is making her way back to him. He jots down a few words to summarize this impending victory and then turns back to the tablet. After all, he knows that this project is merely one of many that need to move forward in order for him to truly prevail.

7

They had warned her that Peter was a *ladies' man*. That he would be an easy target. There would be no cause for concern emotionally because he was the champion of conquests. And while Mandy is by no means a shy person, she'd never gone out intentionally to seduce someone before.

Her job, until recently, was more of a marketing endeavor. An aim to get people less afraid of the ever-popular issue of overcrowding and to reconcile the divide growing between individuals with longer life spans and the populace that don't.

Her most recent campaign focused on the advocation of colonizing nearby planets. The primary argument revolved around the existence of The Air City and its expansive network of Air Colonies. Based on the fact that such technology and know-how exist, she reasoned it was only a matter of time before they would accomplish planetary colonization as well. Mandy even created an entire campaign around the phrase "One small step for man, one giant leap for inclusion." Her favorite part about the campaign was that only those with longevity actually knew where she'd lifted the majority of the quote from. A little inside joke to herself.

Looking out across The City's landscape, Mandy can see one of the smaller signs from this very campaign in a nearby window, the silhouette of a rocket ship contrasted against a deep blue, nearly black backdrop with white dots simulating a starry sky. Seeing this brings Mandy back to the very moment she was first approached for her current *assignment*, as The Director puts it.

It was a perfect day weather-wise, warm with a light

breeze. She had just finished her speech on *Expanding Our Reach* and was now mingling with the crowd, taking questions from those too shy to ask in front of the larger group. It had been no secret she herself was a Near Mortal, and there were always a handful of people curious about that topic alone. Limiting these Q&A sessions to fifteen minutes, Mandy would then excuse herself and be escorted by a large guard in case there were any protesters.

Turning away from the crowd that fateful day, she saw a face that up until then she had only seen on her marketing material. The Director. Even while moving up through the ranks, she nor anyone she'd worked with had ever seen him in person as he only met face-to-face with a small and select group of their staff. He was like the mythical Great and Powerful Oz, leading them forward, but only from behind the scenes. She had honestly figured the images they'd used to depict him were of a random model and that the actual position of Director was all a facade, a story to keep them all going. Yet there he was, with his dark brown hair perfectly groomed and his light blue eyes looking directly at her. She found herself blushing as he approached. She continued to pack up her campaign material and tried to maintain composure, unsure of how she would react if he really started talking to her.

"Mandy," The Director stated as if affirming her name as he reached out his hand to hers. She received it with a firm grip of her own, noting that his shake was perfect—not too strong, but notably confident. "It's a pleasure finally meeting you. I've heard so many outstanding things that I had to come out and see you in action," he continued as he let go of her hand. Mandy was literally speechless.

He's heard about me, she thought with a mix of excitement and dread, but she quickly reminded herself that he came to see her. Enthusiasm pushed the fear out of her way.

The Director then quickly made a motion with his right hand and all of her equipment was taken away by men she hadn't noticed until that very moment. Slightly startled by this action, Mandy tried hard to not let her face reveal the fear that was quietly creeping back in. She was unsure how she recognized none of these men accompanying The Director despite having worked for The Facility for over seven years. It was all so mysterious.

"Let's go somewhere a little less crowded," The Director said while extending his arm for Mandy to take. She took it, noticing her own security guard was now standing a distance away gawking at her. She just shrugged over her shoulder at him and walked away, noticing she was not the only one surprised by The Director's presence. The entire crowd was watching and whispering as Mandy continued walking.

Of course, she thought to herself. *They had to have recognized him immediately. After all, he is the face of The Facility.*

Next thing she knew, they were in a laughably small coffee shop—a literal hole in the wall with only a couple tables, all of which were occupied by members of The Director's entourage she recognized from her bag removal. Mandy and The Director sat at a table in the middle while his team of six turned around so that their backs were to them, a human shield of sorts. Mandy's head was swimming. She had always considered her post as more than just a job. Her coworkers and supervisors were family to her, and this cause was truly *her cause* as a Near Mortal herself. She couldn't count the number of times she'd said that she would do anything for The Facility. Apparently, word got around.

Nonchalantly sipping the coffee that had been waiting for them, Mandy leaned back in her chair, ready to go with the flow. The Director then unloaded the entire plan on her: the train ride, the meeting of her target, acquiring his essence, and, most importantly, the swift departure. With her coffee nearly depleted by the end of his proposal, she transitioned to sipping it slowly, afraid that she might have to talk if she set the cup down.

The Director patiently waited and sipped his own coffee, keeping his stunning blue eyes on her. Down to practically coffee grounds, Mandy finally set her cup down. Unable to find anything else to say, she went with the only thing that kept bouncing around her head.

"A seductress?" she blurted out quizzically.

"That's a perfect phrase for it. Yes," The Director answered. "*A seductress.*"

"Me?" Mandy asked in pure disbelief, bringing her hand to her chest and pointing at herself.

"Absolutely!" he replied enthusiastically.

"But Director—" she protested.

"Please, Mandy. Call me Tian," responded The Director, maintaining direct eye contact with her. This took her aback almost as much as the proposal, but she didn't let it phase her as she was awash with questions.

"Alright, Tian," she began. "So you believe he's truly Immortal then? I mean, I always thought that was just a rumor, someone being truly Immortal. If you're wrong and he's just Near, then me having his child would be a death sentence for me. And honestly, even if he is Immortal, we don't know if it wouldn't also be my demise."

"We are quite sure. He *is* Immortal. And we do understand the risks you'd be taking," Tian replied before pausing to take another sip of his coffee. "But we are—or rather, *I* am—very impressed with all you've done in the brief time you've been with us. You've moved up the ranks at an unheard-of speed. That shows true dedication, that you're not just with us for a job but that you're devoted to us. To the cause."

Mandy stared down at her empty cup, wishing there was even a drop left that she could sip.

"I'd love to tell you to take your time and to think this over," Tian continued. "But we never know when Peter will resurface. We would need you to begin your training by week's end at the latest."

Mandy involuntarily let out a small laugh, immediately covering her mouth. Tian pretended not to notice this outburst.

"I know it's brief notice, but I truly believe that you are the perfect fit for this job. You've been nothing but faithful to us, getting out there and spreading the gospel, so to speak. And you do also fit his, how do I say, dating profile."

Mandy couldn't believe he was actually serious. She knew all the stats. The chances of her surviving delivery were poor at best. And going to meet a man just to get knocked up was one of the most insane things she'd ever heard. Yet there was a large part of her that had to admit being the first woman in history to have a child half-Near and half-Immortal was very tempting, never mind being the first Near Mortal to survive childbirth. Becoming a mother was never something she'd given any thought to, knowing full well her kind and procreation didn't mix, but Tian's proposition stirred a motherly instinct she hadn't known to even exist in herself. Finally, there was an even more substantial part of her that was, as Tian just put it, sincerely devoted to the cause.

"What do you think?" Tian asked with hope and a tinge of impatience in his voice.

Mandy looked up at him and noticed that she'd been sitting in silence longer than she'd realized.

"Of course, there would be more compensation than just the glory of surviving the first Near Mortal baby, of which we could never divulge to anyone," Tian continued, ensuring he'd reeled her in. "But Mandy," Tian stressed in a low tone, leaning in towards her, "there would not only be a financial gain for you from this conquest but also a tremendous bump in title once everything is said and done. How does Director of Recruitment sound?"

Mandy's face remained the same, taking all of the information in at once and unsure of what her next move would be. Off this continued silence, Tian moved to his next offer.

"Really, you can be a lead in any department you're interested in."

There was still no movement from Mandy. She couldn't believe what she was hearing—a shortcut to the position of her dreams. Even with the risk, it was nearly too good to be true.

"Basically," Tian continued, trying to hide his uncertainty

of her answer at this point, "whatever your goal within our organization is, it's yours." With that, Tian picked up his coffee cup and sipped the remainder of the drink, unwilling to plead any more.

Seeing the desire Tian had for her, Mandy gave it another fifteen seconds—not wanting to seem too easy, but also not wanting to have this offer leave the table.

"Well, as you know, this was my last scheduled rally of the season," Mandy smoothly replied, looking Tian straight in the eyes as she spoke. While his intimidation factor had gone down tremendously, a slight shiver still went down her spine with his eye contact. She sighed and then continued, "It would be an honor to take on this mission."

"Perfect!" Tian nearly shouted. "We'll get everything in order," he continued and motioned again with his right hand, signaling for his associates to escort them both out to the square.

The pop of a small firecracker in the distance snaps Mandy out of this now distant memory. Walking towards the sound, a smile crosses her face as she sees small children chasing each other with poppers. Now sitting on the wall, she continues to reflect on that fateful day, remembering how they'd described Peter.

He did not come across as a ladies' man in the least. She had to proposition him. Going over and over the evening in her head, Mandy still is a little lost. All she's sure of at this moment is that she has to get back to The Facility. They need to start the testing to ensure that the seed took, having secured some extra in her small case as a backup.

That will only stay cool for so long, she thinks as she glances over towards the case, hoping that she will see the steam in the air signaling that the train will be at the station soon.

With a sigh, she stares off into the distance before finally seeing it—that faint trail of white. A signal for Mandy to return to the train station. She takes one more deep breath before walking back over to the fire escape, grabbing her case, and making her way back down to the alley, ready to continue back *home*.

8

Peter departs the train and heads straight to the Air Cab depot. He may loathe this form of travel, but deep down Peter enjoys the actual process of hailing a cab. He finds the entire system fairly ingenious. He admires the setup, with each Air Cab queue ending at a call button that links to a docking station miles above. When this button is pressed, the corresponding signal will flash, notifying the cabbie of its pending fare.

To distract himself from the fact that he has to take this flying form of transportation, Peter partakes in his favorite pastime—people watching. He notes almost immediately that most people in line display the same sense of urgency. From the rapid tap of a foot to the repeated push of the call button, they seem to need to keep in continuous motion. As the fastest way to get to any destination on the ground or in the sky, Air Cabs are a magnet for busy people. Even so, it is as if these individuals are in a competition to prove who is the busiest. They make a show of being on their communication devices, repeatedly looking at their timepieces, and tapping their feet just a little faster or louder. The thought of this secret rivalry makes Peter smile.

In contrast to the impatient hustlers are those new to the system of air travel, another category Peter appreciates. These people are easy to pick out, typically boasting either a look of awe or apprehension. The middle-aged woman accompanied by her preteen boy directly behind Peter are a perfect example: the child full of questions and his mother, Peter assumes, patiently answering each one. She explains how the entire Air Cab operation works, from the call buttons to the mechanics behind the levitating machines themselves. Eavesdropping for a moment,

Peter is impressed by her knowledge, thinking she must be at minimum an engineer of some sort.

Moving closer to his current destination, however, these distractions stop working and Peter is reminded of the third category of people in line—the ones who experience the flip side of the excitement that air travel can bring. Dread. When observing these individuals, Peter finds that they will give the call button a quick tap and wait, typically fidgeting as the Air Cab descends upon them. This is the category Peter counts himself in. He isn't afraid to fly, really. It is the traffic that frightens him. Even before The Collision, trusting others in fast-moving vehicles was never something Peter was good at. Then you add to the horizontal landscape of driving not only vertical lanes but sometimes up to four lanes of traffic above and below, and you get a very nervous Peter.

"When is the man in front of us going to push the button?" the boy behind him loudly asks, bringing Peter back to reality. Having gotten lost in his phobia once again, Peter suddenly finds himself next. Shaking off any residual nerves, Peter glances behind him and gives the kid a nervous smile, then hits the bright yellow call button. Fortunately, being near the train station means the line of Air Cabs waiting for a fare is long, making his wait mere moments.

As the Air Cab arrives, the driver, a deeply tan woman in her late sixties, sees Peter's suitcase and pops open the trunk. He waves in appreciation and places the case in the trunk, closes it gingerly, and climbs into the back seat, giving the cabbie directions to his first sale.

They are off before Peter can even put his seatbelt on, jetting straight up. Aside from the traffic, another thing he severely dislikes about Air Cabs are the roofs themselves. Needing to see traffic in every direction, the roofs on all flying vehicles are one giant window. In a lot of ways, Peter wishes that he could be comfortable with this form of travel. He sees not only the logic behind the vehicle's design but how one could find it enjoyable watching this symphony of transportation. At the moment, however, enjoyable is not a word Peter would use to describe this experience, having a front-row seat as vehicles careen past him in every direction.

"You okay back there?" the cabbie asks as she peers back at Peter in the rearview mirror. Realizing his embarrassing little yelps were escaping him each time they made a lane change, Peter clears his throat and straightens himself out.

"Quite fine, thank you. This isn't my first rodeo, I promise," Peter replies to the cabbie with forced confidence and a slight smile. The cabbie chortles, tugging at her cap at this remark.

"It isn't mine either," she responds, returning her focus to the steady flow of traffic.

Adjusting his attention to his internal surroundings, Peter finds that he is in one of the cleanest cabs he's ever seen. He can smell the air freshener hanging from the rearview mirror, a nondescript yet pleasant floral scent. The backseat is spotless, and she even offers him both gum and a bottled water. Feeling a little thirsty, Peter takes the water. After a couple sips and a few deep breaths, he's actually able to relax a little.

"I've just never really gotten used to this form of travel. Sorry about that," he remarks, making eye contact with the driver in the mirror and noting the wrinkles that have permanently settled in around her eyes. "Thank you for the water," he continues, now moving his attention over to the mounted driver's license on the dashboard. "How long have you been driving, Charlotte?" he asks, working on distracting himself enough to stop squeaking.

"Before you were in diapers, young man," Charlotte proclaims, keeping her gaze forward. Peter chuckles but for reasons Charlotte would never understand. Shaking his head, he looks down at his watch and notices he's running a bit late.

"Any way you could get me to my destination in about fifteen minutes?" he inquires. Charlotte looks back at him in the mirror.

"I could, but you'd have to promise me you're not going

to lose your shit," she replies, only half-joking. Peter laughs at this phrase but seriously considers what she's implying for a moment. Taking in the pristine surroundings again and her overall calm and controlled demeanor, Peter decides that he can indeed *keep his shit together*.

"I'm in!" Peter declares, looking straight back at Charlotte in the mirror.

"Alright! Hold on back there!" Charlotte howls, switching her controls from automatic to manual. "And no more yelping," she teases as she tosses her cap in the seat next to her, causing her long red hair to cascade down her back. "This is gonna be fun!" she mutters more to herself than Peter as she leans forward in her seat.

The sight makes Peter begin to reconsider his decision, but he can tell it's already too late to change his mind as he watches her size up the traffic, looking for holes and opportunities. Even with his fears, Peter is impressed with the way Charlotte takes each and every opportunity, weaving in and out of the multiple lanes of traffic like a seamstress.

Although he's able to keep his yelps to himself, Peter finds that white knuckles are not off the table, nor potentially a little pee as well by the time they pull up to the destination. Touching down, Peter is relieved by the fact that he is not only on time but a few minutes ahead of schedule. Using cash from his dwindling stash, Peter pays the fare, leaving a large tip to show his appreciation for the skilled driving and that they made it in one piece.

"Thanks for getting me here in time," Peter stammers as he pours himself out of the cab and retrieves his suitcase from the trunk, knowing that while he may be Immortal, pain is still pain.

"Thank you!" Charlotte replies. "I never get to drive like that anymore. Really took me back to my racing days," she adds with a smile and a wink as she takes off, merging once again into the flow of traffic and leaving Peter with the image of her red hair blowing in the wind.

9

Piles and piles of bodies, near but not quite dead.

Never dead.

All silent.

Falling silent years ago.

Buried miles below the earth's surface in bunker-like storage rooms.

People above going about their business.

No one aware of the horrors below.

No one but The Director.

The Director's triumph.

The Director, finally getting the world back on course.

His course.

Standing at the entrance of his below-ground salvation, able to view his glory.

His conquest.

Finally able to rest.

The impenetrable black of the underground tomb is contrasted by the vivacious white flames of the candlelit atmosphere, stirring a nearly romantic feeling for Tian. Shadows of himself looking down upon all the work he has accomplished, all the vermin finally cleaned out of his society, swirl around in his mind. Even the odor of sweet decay seems to linger in Tian's nose as a knock on his upper-office door startles him awake.

"Yes?" Tian utters, the last few images from his dream still echoing in his head as a slender man in his early twenties peeks his head in the room. Seeing that he has disturbed The Director, the young aide visibly tenses, explaining himself in a hurried pace.

"Sorry, sir, I didn't mean to—"

"It's fine," Tian cuts off the apology. He sits straight up and rubs the sleep out of his eyes with one hand, then looks straight at this gentleman. "Yes?" he asks with a heavy dose of annoyance in his voice as the aide has yet to explain this disturbance.

"Mandy, sir. She's on board the train and set to arrive at The Facility on schedule," reports the aide in the same rushed tone.

"Perfect!" Tian responds, putting his hands behind his head and leaning back in his chair. A couple more seconds go by. The aide remains, standing perfectly still. "Was there something else?" Tian asks, raising an eyebrow.

"Oh! No, sir. Sorry, sir," he answers immediately. "I just thought there would be a message, or..." The aide stops himself midsentence, turns, and exits swiftly, closing the door behind him without a sound.

On the subterranean level, Tian has under his employment some of the most brilliant scientists and military men and women working for him, but the volunteers on the upper level are a far cry from smart, let alone brilliant. But in their loyalty they all are beyond committed. Not only to the cause of unification between races, but more importantly, to the cause's leader. Which is precisely what Tian needs. Loyalty. Truly, the fact that most are more than a stone's throw away from bright and a majority lack basic common sense doesn't hurt either.

The easier to control them by, Tian reasons.

The uncertainty of Mandy's detour does have him slightly concerned. Questions begin to bubble up to the surface with this new check-in. Is she still on their side? Had she set up some kind of meeting between the seduction of Peter and her scheduled return to The Facility? The mere fact that she is now returning on time unsettles him more than the initial news of her premature departure. This shows forethought. She knew she would have time for this detour.

As more questions build in his head, Tian writes each one down, scribbling out every concern until he runs out of room on the sheet of lined paper. Being able to physically see these worries refocuses Tian, reminding him that he already anticipated that Mandy would need time to reflect after her deed was done. And if there is one fact he knows about Mandy, it is that she would never endanger *her cause*. In the end, she is his girl. The one he chose to carry out the conception. She's his exception to the rule when it comes to smart upper-level workers.

Feeling more secure in his plan, Tian takes the sheet of worries, crumples it into a tight ball, and tosses it in the trash, ready to continue with his day. He knows he is in control, and from Plan A to Z he shall remain so.

Even with this self-assured thinking, Tian finds his thoughts immediately turn back towards Mandy's departure. Picking his pen back up, he looks at the fresh sheet of paper as his landline rings. Glancing at the caller ID, Tian sees the name of his right-hand man. *Sergeant Region*. Tian is grateful for the interruption and picks up immediately.

"Hello, Sergeant," Tian answers. "I'm assuming you heard the wonderful news."

"Yes, sir," Sergeant Region replies in his formal tone. "I'm calling to confirm you still want to go ahead with Plan B."

"Yes," Tian says with a slight pause. "I actually think I've figured out a way to combine the two plans, keeping them both more stable in the process," Tian continues, beginning to doodle on the notepad in front of him.

"Glad to hear it, sir," Sergeant Region responds plainly.

"Indeed!" Tian asserts more forcefully than intended. "Come up to my office in thirty and I'll fill you in on our new objective. We can call it Plan A-B-A."

"*ABBA*, sir?" Sergeant Region asks, pronouncing the acronym with an inflection not typical for him.

"I just heard it," Tian responds before pausing again. "Let's just skip ahead and call it Plan C."

"Plan C it is, sir. I'll be up in thirty," Sergeant Region states.

"Perfect," Tian concludes with a slight smile, finishing up his drawing.

Hanging up the receiver, he finds his thoughts are no longer focused on Mandy and her odd detour, but rather on his earlier dream about his triumph. The image he is now putting the finishing touches on depicts this victory.

A victory he can now taste.

10

Mandy boards this train with much less excitement than the last time and heads straight to the open seating section where she takes the first seat she finds. Her time to reflect was not nearly as helpful as she'd hoped, and now her thoughts are divided between her recent conquest and the continuation of her mission. On top of this, Mandy is the definition of exhausted, having not slept in over forty-eight hours. She tries to convince herself otherwise by adjusting her posture and stretching out her legs.

Knowing there will be no time to sleep in her upcoming schedule, Mandy gets up and goes to the dining car, straight to the bar, and orders a double espresso and a sizeable piece of chocolate cake. The mix of caffeine and sugar will allow her to stay awake until she can finally be back in her room and, most importantly, in her bed. Of course, there are still a number of tests that stand between her and her bed. Lamenting this fact with a sigh, she takes her purchased goodies back to her seat.

Looking out the window, Mandy views the familiar urban landscape swiftly passing by. Looking up, she can see the underbellies of lower Air Cars as they speed by and in between the flow of Air City traffic, that ever-present structure looming in the distance. A goal to many of the people she grew up with, and for her both an asset and an enemy. Although the additional space did initially calm those that would turn on her race for their longevity, The Air City also acts as a safe haven for the majority of people against her cause. She knows this kind of thinking— grouping an enormous mass of individuals into one category— is the exact thing she fights against, but it is hard not to when so much evidence is there. Proof that those living in the air are more likely to vote against and try to put an end to her people's very existence than those living in the urban sprawl on the land.

Looking back to her treat, Mandy works her way out of this unproductive thinking and finds that by the time she's done eating they're already at her stop, much faster than she'd expected. With this small gift of time, Mandy can now take a rickshaw back to The Facility instead of an Air Cab, which she hates. Fortunately, most of her fellow travelers are in line for the Air Cabs, so hailing her own rickshaw is an easy endeavor.

Quickly hopping into the back of the first open one she sees, Mandy gives the driver the address for The Facility and off they go. Some may find this form of travel dangerous, but Mandy absolutely adores it. Both the size of the vehicle and the boldness of the driver make her giddy as they weave in and out of traffic, truly feeling *in* The City. While she still delivers the occasional speech, her time these days mainly consists of being at a desk indoors, so zooming in and out of neighborhoods is pure pleasure.

Pulling up to The Facility, she pays the rickshaw driver in cash, grabs her case, and walks up the steps. Still hours away from nightfall, there will be plenty of debriefing and several tests before she can finally collapse. Her entire body feels heavy with fatigue at the thought of this as Mandy opens one of the entrance's glass double doors and passes through to the front desk. She waits for the receptionist to come over and talk to her, a slight smile gracing her face as she remembers one perk of this assignment is getting a room to herself. Her sleep tonight will be utterly and completely uninterrupted.

A heavyset woman in her late fifties lumbers towards the desk, returning from a storage area in the back.

"Hi, Fawn," Mandy sings with a lyrical cadence.

"Hey, Mandy," Fawn replies, dropping the supplies she had gathered behind the desk. "Did you need some help?" she asks with a wide grin.

"Can you please let Ti—The Director know that I'm here?" she asks as coolly as possible, knowing that Fawn would find this request unusual at best.

"The Director?" she clarifies with more than a little surprise in her voice.

"Yes, please," Mandy answers, trying not to sound condescending. Choosing not to push the point, Fawn picks up the desk's landline and presses the one. Holding the receiver to her ear, she maintains an ever-growing grin. After a minute of ringing, Fawn hangs up.

"Sorry, no answer," Fawn reports plainly to Mandy without letting her smile drop. Disappointed in this news, Mandy takes a second to regroup. She doesn't want to stand in the lobby any longer than necessary, as she is sure there are a multitude of rumors about her flying around.

"Can you try one more time?" asks Mandy in a tone that doesn't allow for anything but a yes. Fawn complies, picking up the receiver and dialing once again, this time making a show of looking at her watch and then to the packages waiting for her attention. After another minute of ringing, Fawn places the receiver back on its stand.

"Sorry, still no answer," Fawn smugly reports. "You can wait over there," she continues, motioning to the waiting area and its two broken-down chairs.

Mandy just nods at Fawn with a forced smile, then turns away and starts walking towards the hallway to The Director's office.

"Mandy!" Fawn calls after her, but Mandy pays no mind. She's gone too far to let a little thing like an unanswered phone stop her from quickly debriefing and getting to her new suite.

11

Being a tad early thanks to Charlotte, Peter takes a leisurely stroll through a couple of adjacent neighborhoods on his way to his first drop of the day. Peter particularly enjoys looking at the wide variety of architecture built next to each other. Many people within the wealthier communities try to separate themselves from the rest of the population by bringing back classic architectural styles. This creates not only a divide between the haves and have-nots but also a real eyesore. Having an eighteenth-century castle right up next to an A-frame followed by a log cabin facade, it's like walking through an architect's fever dream.

Even as an eyesore, Peter finds each home amusing at the very least and some of them even beautiful. Arriving at the address Jonah gave him, Peter finds a very narrow and tall apartment complex that looks like it had been built as an afterthought following the construction of the two neighboring homes. He's almost forgotten that while this is a wealthy neighborhood, there is always room for some affordable housing squeezed into every corner of The City. *Alley homes*, as they are referred to. That would also explain the address's digits, 1300 ¾, Peter muses as he approaches the front entryway.

The fact that his client lives in this building does not surprise Peter, as a significant portion of the people who purchase his goods are not all that well-to-do. More often than not, Peter finds that the commodities he sells are a means of escapism for his customers. True, these artifacts are not cheap, but they are still cost-effective compared to getting an ocular implant or going out to see live events, which only take place in The Air City these days.

Hopping up the handful of stairs to the wrought iron gate, Peter notices a rusty call button covered in cobwebs. He presses down hard but it barely budges. The button doesn't light up or buzz, so he gives the front gate a pull. It opens with a loud squeal, notifying the residents that there is a guest, the unattended hinges working as well as any buzzer would. Glancing down at the piece of wrinkled paper in his hand, he makes his way to the address given, noting that each front door is a part of a quarter system.

Coming upon a bright red door with the numbers 1300 ¾ on it, Peter double-checks the address and knocks. A rustling noise immediately comes from the other side, followed by the darkening of the peephole and then the familiar sound of a dead-bolt and a number of additional security measures unlocking. As the door slowly opens, Peter sees the pleasantly round face of a tiny woman with curly silver hair.

"Ms. Liana, I presume?" Peter asks with a smile and extends his hand.

"Yes! You must be Peter," the woman replies, opening the door much wider. She eagerly places her tiny hand into his, enthusiastically shaking it while looking him up and down. "Please come in," Liana says, motioning for Peter to follow her as she scurries back in and disappears down a small, narrow hallway. He follows her lead through this little tunnel of an entrance, ending up in a sunken den. Peter chooses the closest seat he sees, sets his case on it, and unpacks her goods.

Liana returns moments later with two cups of water, handing one to Peter and setting hers down on the coffee table. She pulls the other chair in the room directly across from him. Sitting down, her attention quickly turns to the contents he has unpacked for her to inspect. Excitement overwhelms her as she reaches out for the plastic-covered volume, hands shaking a little as she holds it in her lap.

"I just can't. How do you have this?" she inquires as she looks down at the comic, a first edition of *The Fantastic Four*.

"I'm just a lucky collector. Speaking of..." Peter trails off as he takes out a signed picture of the author. "I like to add this to all my orders, just as a nice little treat," he states as he hands the photo over to Liana, who takes it graciously and then stands up, placing both of her new items on the coffee table far away from her cup of water.

"This is too much! I can't just—" Liana breaks off and heads down one of the hallways.

While left alone, Peter has a moment to truly take in the home. It is, in his opinion, quite spectacular. It reminds him of the center of a gerbil habitat, with its round, tunnellike hallways taking off in all directions. The decor of the room pays homage to the genre he sells the most. Any wall space available is lined with graphic novels and comic books, most in plastic or the original packaging. He wonders if she even reads them or if she is one of those who just needs to own.

Returning moments later with her purse, Liana rejoins Peter in the den.

"At least let me pay you more for this," she says while gesturing to the signed picture and then dives deep into her bag, almost disappearing into it.

"No, really, it's my gift to you. Just think about ordering again from me in the future. That's all I ask," Peter replies with a boyish grin. Resurfacing from her purse, she begins counting out the money.

"That goes without saying. You are much kinder than any of the others I've dealt with. But you know, this would be much easier if you had a scanner," she expresses as she finishes her double count. "Cash is pretty hard to come by these days."

"And yet I'm betting it's worth all the trouble," Peter replies with a crooked smile. This makes her giggle a little as she hands over her payment to Peter. "Well, I've got more deliveries to make," Peter states as he stands up. "It really was a pleasure doing business with you." She escorts him to the door, thanking him more times than he can count and shaking his hand once more before allowing him to depart.

Amongst the architectural hodgepodge again, he's glad

that his next appointment is close enough to walk to and that his first appointment went smooth enough to allow him time to do so. Starting the journey to this next home, he pauses for a moment to admire a ranch house. Peter takes a deep breath in. It excites him that he's one appointment down. Only two more sales to go. Then he can return to his reclusive ways until Jonah, once again, requests his services.

12

Mandy heads straight to Tian's office, excited to report that she was the perfect secret agent. Getting closer to the door, however, she can hear that he's not alone. She recognizes the second voice as Sergeant Region. She continues forward but stops short when she hears Peter's name. After a few seconds, she shrugs this off as her two superiors talking about her mission and continues to the door. Giving it a quick knock, Mandy pushes the ajar door open, stopping the two gentlemen midsentence.

"No need to stop on my account," Mandy declares as she enters the room. Both men stare at her, unsure of how much she's heard. After a brief and awkward moment of silence, Tian breaks the tension.

"Mandy!" he cheers and quickly gets to his feet to walk over to her. He greets her with a firm handshake, taking the case from her with his other hand simultaneously. Sergeant Region stays still.

"I'm back and ready to be debriefed, sir," she says in a mock-military voice as the handshake ends. Tian laughs at this.

"Slow down a little, Mandy. There's plenty of time for all that tomorrow. Today we're just happy that you're back," he assures her as he returns to his desk. "I'll have Karen come up front and take you to the lab to run some preliminary tests, but then it's off to dinner and bed. Tomorrow we can go over much more," Tian finishes, sitting back down behind his desk and setting the case directly next to him.

Mandy is relieved by this information, as she's a step beyond weary and ready to have an entire evening to herself. Images of a comfy bed begin to run through her head.

"Sounds perfect to me, sir," Mandy replies, prompting smiles from both gentlemen.

Tian reaches for his desk phone and dials Karen, asking her to meet Mandy in the front lobby and take her to the lab for the initial tests that have been set up. There is a moment of silence as Mandy looks from Tian to the sergeant and then back to Tian, both men staring at her, their smiles becoming more forced with each passing second.

"I'll just head off to the lobby then, sir," Mandy states, feeling incredibly awkward.

Tian nods with a smile. A smile that sends a slight shiver down Mandy's spine. Trying to not let the sensation show externally, she exits quickly. Pausing for a moment just outside the door, hoping to catch more of the conversation she walked in on earlier. Hearing nothing, she continues down the hall to the front desk where Fawn still sits manning the entrance.

"He was there after all," Mandy quips in Fawn's direction as she passes the desk and continues towards Karen, who is already standing patiently in the waiting area. "Karen," Mandy says as they briefly embrace. "It's been far too long," she continues, following Karen out of the lobby and down the hallway Mandy has always associated with her annual checkups.

"Tian does know how to keep a girl busy," Karen replies with a straight face, which only makes both women laugh even harder.

"That's one way to put it," Mandy squeezes out between her remaining giggles. When their laughter dies down, it dawns on Mandy that she doesn't actually know who all the people *in the know* really are regarding her mission.

Does Karen know? she thinks to herself as they walk momentarily in silence. There had been a list of approved individuals, and a cover story of course, but there are already things happening that she didn't expect. Sergeant Region, for example, being in Tian's office. Or Karen, one of her closest associates at The Facility, being the one to bring her down to the medical center. Her thoughts then jump to the next big question. *Why am I being escorted?* Mandy knows full well where her tests will take place. *So what's with the extra support?* she ponders as Karen breaks the silence.

"It really has been too long, Mandy. It's funny that in such a small community like ours that we can still go so long without running into each other," Karen finishes with a smile as she looks over at Mandy, who returns with a smile of her own.

Is she trying to get information out of me? Mandy's growingly paranoid brain asks. But out loud she responds with, "Right! That's what you get for choosing to live in the South Wing. I warned you from day one, choose your wing and you choose your posse."

Karen breaks out in laughter again. Mandy tries to join and manages a chuckle.

"You were right. I am a South Sider for sure," Karen responds through her laughter as they arrive at the medical office.

Mandy goes to open the door labeled *Clinic* but finds that it's locked and now she's fallen behind. She speeds up her pace to catch up to Karen farther down the hall. Karen seems oblivious to Mandy's attempt to enter the locked room. Not wanting to seem out of the loop, Mandy refrains from asking where exactly they are going but becomes even more suspicious with every step they take away from the regular clinic.

"Regardless of North Wings and South Wings, we really should catch up soon," Karen continues. "Maybe we could brunch," she finishes as they make a right, going down a hallway Mandy has never been through before. Mandy finally understands why Karen is here to lead her.

They soon arrive at a plain white door. Karen lightly knocks and opens the door, revealing a small yet fully equipped medical lab. As they both walk in, Mandy is taken aback by the amount of equipment one small room can hold. Not knowing a lot about scientific equipment, she is intrigued by all the machinery.

"Hello," comes a woman's voice, making Mandy jump a little as she hadn't noticed the woman standing in the corner.

Holding a clipboard, this tall, slim, blond woman motions for Mandy to take a seat at what looks like a drawing station.

Mandy and Karen greet the woman as Mandy crosses over to the seat, resting her right arm on the padded armrest.

"Perfect," Karen says to no one in particular, clasping her hands together. The blond woman gathers a basket full of test tubes, crosses over to Mandy, and begins methodically laying them out on a silver tray table. Mandy looks over at Karen, whose face has quickly drained of color.

"I can take it from here," Mandy says to her. "I know my way back."

"If you're sure," Karen murmurs almost halfway out the door.

"Yes. I'll be fine," Mandy assures Karen.

"Okay. We'll do brunch soon," she blurts out with a forced smile and exits.

"Grab hold of this and pump," the blond woman says in a straightforward and professional tone to Mandy. Mandy does as she's told, curious how there is yet another person working at The Facility she doesn't know.

"I don't think I got your name," Mandy says as the woman finishes laying out the various tubes that will be filled today. Looking up at Mandy, the woman seems as if she's just been snapped out of a daydream.

"I guess you're right," she replies, brightening her disposition a little. "I'm sorry, I just get so wrapped up in making sure I have all the right…" she apologizes before cutting herself off. She pauses for a moment and then continues. "I'm Elysabeth," she finishes before slowly taking a deep breath, focused now on Mandy.

"It's nice to officially meet you," Mandy responds, offering her left hand across her body to shake. With a giggle, Elysabeth receives it.

"Nice to officially meet you as well, Mandy," she returns. "Seems like we'll be seeing a lot of each other in the next eight months and some change," Elysabeth continues with a warm grin that calms Mandy enough for her to not even notice the initial prick of the needle entering her arm.

13

"So that's the *stuff*?" Sergeant Region inquires, motioning with his head towards the case sitting next to Tian.

"Indeed, it is. Life-giving juice, if you will," Tian replies, trying to get a rise out of his cohort. Not taking the bait, Sergeant Region quickly changes the subject.

"And the bird has come home to roost. Now we just need the one in the bush to make it a happy family." Tian laughs despite himself.

"I love it when you mix metaphors," he chuckles before pausing and straightening himself up a little. "But in all seriousness, we do need to get the bird in the bush's location nailed down." Sergeant Region nods in agreement. Tian waits for more of a response, but he gets none. "Was there anything else you needed for Plan C?" he asks, picking up a pen and making a show of needing to get back to his work at hand.

"No, sir. I will make sure the new cell is ready and that we have more than enough security detail for the extra shifts," Sergeant Region answers, walking towards the door.

"Perfect. Just so long as everything is ready for our expected guest," Tian says, looking up at his second-in-command with an icy smile.

"It will be," Sergeant Region responds, then departs.

Tian sets the pen down and turns to the progress reports on his computer, thinking about the fact that this could be his last calm night for quite a while. Mandy, his primary concern, is taken care of for the evening. With this, Tian decides to take this moment and duck out early. He has a backlog of virtual entertainment waiting for him, and the idea of a solid night's sleep is in sight now that his bird is indeed home. Locking the door to his upper office, Tian heads out the back exit, not wanting to run into any reason to keep him later.

14

Approaching his second client's home, Peter immediately notes the difference in location. This patron lives not in an alley home but rather a massive apartment complex, one that takes up several city blocks. Peter double-checks the number of the apartment before going up to the shiny metallic box and pressing the call button. Moments later, a response cracks through the copper speaker.

"Yes?" comes a feminine voice.

"It's Peter here with your order!" he shouts in the box's direction.

A high-pitched *Bzzzzzzzz* comes from the gate directly next to the call box. Peter grabs for the brass doorknob before the noise stops and pulls the heavy, exquisitely designed door towards him. While doing so he notes not only how clean this gate is, as he's able to see his reflection in the large brass slats, but also the carvings within these slats depicting delicate flowers curving around each other.

Continuing forward, Peter looks for a directory to lead him in the address's direction, noticing almost immediately a large sign providing him the correct numeric trajectory. He follows this arrow and then the corresponding smaller signs counting down to his goal location. He takes a good fifteen minutes to navigate this colossal structure, passing several vending machines, laundry rooms, and a couple of gyms on the way. Finally, he arrives at the correct door. After checking the address once more, Peter gives the door a knock. He is immediately received by the door swinging open, revealing an older woman wearing a pink tracksuit with her jet-black hair pulled back in a high ponytail.

"I'm Peter," he says while extending his hand to introduce himself. The woman takes his hand in hers, shaking it briefly.

"Marsha," she replies. "Won't you come in?" she continues, allowing him passage into her home. The layout of the apartment is much more open than his previous appointment's. The entryway leads directly into a sitting room that features floor-to-ceiling windows displaying an urban view, a cozy fireplace bookended by two overstuffed armchairs, and, most notably, a wall of books. This isn't a large bookshelf holding books, but rather a wall of books stacked on top of each other. Not stacked horizontally, as if created by a hoarder, but vertically, as if designed by a puzzle master.

Marsha leaves Peter in the sitting room to get them both some water. Peter sets his case down on the coffee table and heads straight to the books, curious about this wall's construction. Upon closer inspection, Peter sees that there are thin sheets of clear plastic shelving between each layer of books. He also notes that he is obviously not the first to bring a rare piece of fiction into this home.

"It's my little obsession," Marsha professes, returning with two glasses of water. "I started collecting at a young age, finding them in old shops here and there. The twentieth century is my favorite era for these works of art. The storytelling was so fresh back then." She is now standing beside him. "Newer stuff either tries to replicate it or outdo it. Neither is ever a success. Don't you think?" she asks as she hands him the glass. Taking the water from her, Peter becomes aware that she is no longer merely standing next to him. She's now pressing up against him, the entire right side of her body flush up against his left.

"I completely agree with you," Peter remarks, slowly and gently removing his body from hers. He then heads back towards his suitcase to dig for the sales item.

The delicate smell of dandelion wafts over him as he looks up from his bag to find Marsha standing directly above him. Her face lights up upon seeing the volume she's ordered, and she holds out her hands longingly. Peter, relieved that any attention he'd been receiving from her is now focused on the publication, gladly goes to hand it over.

"Oh!" Marsha exclaims and turns towards the over-stuffed chairs. "Please just set the book down on the coffee table," she directs over her shoulder, now reaching under one of the arm-chairs and retrieving a pair of white gloves.

A true sign of a collector, Peter thinks as Marsha puts the gloves on and then retrieves the book from the table, slowly lowering herself down onto one of the chairs. After a few moments of inspection, she resurfaces from the book.

"I'm terribly sorry, I'm being rude! I will put my reading aside," Marsha states as she stands back up, setting the book down on the table along with the white gloves.

"Don't be silly," Peter replies. "You've gotta be sure of the merchandise."

"That I will be," she says as she crosses to the other side of the room and removes a hollowed-out book. Trying to give her some privacy regarding this hiding place, Peter bends over and gets into his case. He retrieves the same signed picture he gives all his clients, standing back up just in time to see Marsha turn back around.

There are two things Peter notices immediately. First is the cash he's requested for the book, a large wad in her right hand. Then a very, *very* close second is the fact that the top half of her pink tracksuit is no longer zipped.

As she struts back towards him, Peter grips the picture he has in his hands. Marsha lets her silky raven hair down, shaking her head from one side to the other. The motion draws attention to her breasts as they are barely held into their bright pink home, remarkably perky for their age. Involuntarily shaking his own head, Peter nearly loses his grip on the picture. Backing up, he runs into one of the chairs and plops down.

"Here is a gift I give to my clients for their loyalty," he barely gets out as he extends the photo out to her. She takes the picture in her hand, tosses it over to the other chair, and straddles him. Peter's hands fall to his sides. Even though he is attracted to this woman, Peter finds no carnal response stirring in his body. His mind is still on The Wolf.

Marsha goes in for a tease kiss, hovering so close to his lips she can feel his breath, but breath is all she feels. After a moment she begrudgingly notes this lack of participation. Without a word she zips up her top, stands back up, and stomps down the hallway, leaving Peter alone.

Peter rushes to pack up his case the moment she disappears, cramming the money with the other stack he received earlier in the day. He then gives it a one-two count and heads towards the exit.

"I hope I didn't offend you, Marsha," he calls after her down the hall she retreated to. "I just don't really... well, you know... with clients. It can be bad for business."

No sound comes from the hallway.

"I do have one more appointment today and really must be on my way," he continues, hesitating now at the hallway. Peter takes in one more deep breath and turns to leave, but he suddenly feels a sharp pain in his neck followed by a woozy sensation.

Then black. Collapsing as two women stand over him.

15

An evening at home, Tian thinks to himself as he bursts through the front door. Free time is something Tian rarely gets, and he is ready to make the most of it. Emptying his pockets into the dedicated bowl on the side table next to the front door, he heads straight to his office, needing somewhere safe to store the case that Mandy brought him. Having snuck out so quickly, he didn't have time to drop it off in his underground office and will take no chances with this pivotal sample.

Tian pauses after plugging the case in. The gadget is not only a vintage-looking suitcase but a powerful freezing device as well. He pauses for a moment, considering the substance in this case. Life in its truest form. And, if Mandy can bring this mission to completion, the fuel to power his greatest plan to date.

More than satisfied with himself, Tian leaves his home office and heads to the living room, making a quick detour in the kitchen to grab a half-full bag of sunflower seeds and a bowl for the shells. He sets the bowl in his lap and his bag next to him on the couch, turning his ocular implant on just in time to catch his alma mater's cricket match.

Settling in, he only lasts a few moments before he is fast asleep, having slept only a few hours per night the last few weeks in anticipation of his plan playing out. Even the bowl crashing to the ground does not stir him, needing this dreamless night of sleep to power him up for the coming days.

16

"You just had to bring out the girls, didn't you?" the taller and slightly younger woman scoffs at Marsha.

"Well look at him, Jane," Marsha replies, grabbing Peter under the arms. "You know my game has always been *seductress*. I couldn't help but give it a try, could I?" she continues with a wink as they drag him across the wood floor and heave him onto one of the chairs.

"Better hope The Director doesn't hear about this or your little setup here might vanish," Jane scolds.

"Well, I'm not going to tell him, so I guess I'll know who to go after if ever this gets spread through the grapevine," Marsha replies pointedly.

"You know I'd never," Jane quickly retorts.

"Right. You're just saying," Marsha says sharply, then taps her right temple twice to connect to their home base.

"Is it done?" a flat male voice asks, not allowing Marsha even a simple greeting.

"Yes, we have him," Marsha responds, glancing over at Peter. "He's out cold. Where do you need us to take him?"

"Our men are already on their way to you," the voice replies and disconnects the line. Marsha turns to her accomplice.

"They're on their way."

"Will they be here soon?" Jane asks.

"In such a hurry to leave my company, are you?" Marsha replies, raising an eyebrow.

"It's not that, I just—" Jane scrambles to find her words.

"I'm just teasing you," Marsha says, allowing her companion to ease up a bit. "And yes, they'll be here soon." The other woman takes a seat in the chair across from Peter, who is twitching a little like a dog dreaming about chasing a rabbit.

"He is sort of cute, isn't he?" Jane comments, leaning over and pushing Peter's hair out of his face.

"Thus the attempt, my dear. I don't try to seduce every man that comes through my door." A look of disbelief from Jane and sarcasm from Marsha is exchanged and they both begin to laugh. An abrupt knock at the door interrupts their bonding moment, and Marsha walks over to let in two large gentlemen with a dolly and an antique Oriental rug.

They quickly unroll the rug, revealing the delicate pattern and swirls of reds and oranges that this particular rug comprises. The sight brings Marsha back to her youth, remembering a rug that looked just like this one in her grandmother's home growing up. Wanting to feel the softness of the material, Marsha puts her hand out to touch the rug.

The larger of the two men immediately swats her hand away.

"This is not to be touched by anyone but us, ma'am. We are under strict orders."

Backing away, she stands with her companion and watches as the two men stand Peter up, wrap him in this exquisite rug, place him on the dolly, and wheel him away.

17

Released from the lab and a little light-headed from blood loss, Mandy makes her way straight to the dining hall. She needs a quick snack to get her strength back, and then it's finally off to bed. As she approaches the mess hall, she hears a murmur different from the usual collection of individual conversations. The voices clamor and bounce off one another, sounding more like one unified discussion. Nearing the entrance, Mandy makes out enough words to confirm that the group conversation is about her, and the room falls silent the second Mandy walks in.

All eyes are on her.

Rethinking the need for a quick bite, she turns to go. But before she can run away her best friend Sasha appears next to her. Sasha takes Mandy arm in arm, taps the side of her temple three times to turn on her external speaker, and plays a comical record scratch, breaking the tension in the room. Mandy, more than a little relieved, enjoys the humorous respite.

People gather around the pair as they make their way towards the meal line, shooting questions at Mandy from every direction.

"Just ignore them," Sasha says, literally putting her hand on the face of one of the women coming a tad too close and pushing her away. "You hungry?" she asks as she grabs a couple pieces of fruit from a display.

"Those will do," Mandy replies, ready to take leave.

"Perfect," Sasha responds as they do a quick one-eighty, leaving all the noise behind and heading off to Mandy's new room assignment.

"I've gotta admit, it's gonna be strange not rooming together anymore," Sasha says as she gives Mandy's arm a brief squeeze. "I already have a new roommate, and she's not nearly as cooperative as you."

"That's an interesting adjective to use," Mandy remarks, looking over at Sasha with a slight grin and raised eyebrow.

"Well, you are!" Sasha quips. "Always game for whatever shenanigans are afoot. This one, not so much," Sasha sighs as they arrive at the main lobby elevator. She pushes the up button and looks over at Mandy. "But I suppose that's what makes us besties and not just roomies."

"I suppose so," Mandy acknowledges. She'd been so excited about her solo room, as it was part of the deal she signed when taking this assignment, that Mandy had given no thought to letting go of her roommate. Now standing here next to Sasha, she finds herself having second thoughts. Not that she could back out of her new accommodations, but loneliness had never entered the equation before this moment. As the elevator doors open, Mandy begins to consider the fact that she will not only be in an entirely different wing from Sasha and all of her other friends but an entirely separate floor away. Noticing her friend unable to hide these thoughts from appearing on her face, Sasha quickly rushes to cheer Mandy up.

"Hey! Don't be sad! I was only teasing you. I would never let you off the hook so easily!" Sasha exclaims and gives Mandy a quick squeeze. They both step in the elevator and Sasha presses the button for the top floor. "You can't escape my plans for entertainment. If anything, you having a solo room will only make it easier for us. No one to hide from, just you and me."

"And The Director," Mandy adds.

"Huh?" Sasha cocks her head to one side, reminiscent of a puppy.

"And The Director," she says again plainly. "He said that he would check in on my progress often."

"Oh. Well then, we'll keep our secret stash in the same place. But even so, we'll see each other all the time. I promise."

"So, we still have the stash?" Mandy counters, a smile

beginning to appear on her face.

"Shhh!" Sasha jokingly hushes Mandy.

"But you just brought it up!" Mandy replies in protest.

"Yes, but mine is more theoretic—oh, never mind. It doesn't matter. What does matter is that you're going to have a spectacular view, and I plan to take advantage of it quite often."

This makes Mandy's smile widen, both at the idea of this new view and also at the thought of her friend genuinely following through and coming to visit her.

18

Peter awakes with a kink in his neck and a splitting headache. He's blindfolded but doesn't need sight to know his location. It isn't his first time here, although it's been quite a few years since last they'd *secured* him, as he's heard them refer to it. This he had been grateful for. Anytime he resurfaces to make money, he knows that being taken in is a possibility.

"Hello, Peter," comes a man's voice. The room echoes so much that Peter can't quite make out which direction the voice is coming from. But he knows exactly to whom it belongs.

"Tian? Is that you?" Peter calls out with a warm and sarcastic tone. "I thought you'd be long dead by now. Better be careful. Hang around too long and they'll start to think you're more like me than you might want." Peter moves his head around, trying to pinpoint exactly where Tian is. "What's with the theatrics? It's not like this is my first time visiting you and your lovely thugs."

Peter hears a shuffle of footsteps as more people enter the room, and his head follows the direction of movement while his blindfold is removed. Peter sees two lackeys in the room's rear, with Tian directly in front of him standing close to another man he doesn't recognize in a three-piece suit. The way this unknown man stares Peter down makes him more nervous than usual. The unmoving stillness and deep eyes of this new character make Peter relieved that he's already gotten out of the magnetic cuffs on his wrists, a skill he learned after his first *visit* with Tian.

"Alright guys, you got me. Again," Peter continues with his sarcastic tone, trying not to let any of his nervous energy show. "What's it going to be this time? More tests, perhaps?"

Nothing.

"I do have more appointments to get to today, although kudos on using my line of work to secure me. You definitely crossed a line, but I will admit, I didn't see it coming," Peter rambles, trying to get some kind of response.

Tian and his mysterious guest remain still, but one of the two men in the back quickly ducks into an adjoining room, returning almost immediately with a burlap sack and a small black box.

"Gentlemen?" Peter's voice goes a little higher with concern.

The man hands the black box over to Tian and the sack to the man in the suit before returning to the back of the room. Anxious and realizing they may be his only weapons for the time being, Peter takes the cuffs that had been used to restrain him and hopes that they will add enough impact when he's within striking distance.

The man in the suit whispers something to Tian. They both nod and the nameless man turns to leave, handing the sack to one of the men in the back as he exits. Peter continues his chatter, hoping the distraction will work in his favor.

"Well, glad he's gone. Didn't really get the team-player vibe from him, and I know how important your team is to you," Peter says to Tian, who removes a syringe from the black box before passing the box itself to one of his men.

"I've already had my vaccinations, thank you," Peter reacts to this sight while working on sounding as confident as possible, not enjoying this new theatrical side of Tian one bit. Peter leans slightly back in his chair in anticipation of their next move.

Tian gives Peter a smile. A content smile that conveys to Peter there's something he's missing. Prepared to lunge forward, Peter notices that Tian and his thugs are all just out of striking distance. Tian sees Peter's face reflect this realization and his Cheshire cat smile widens.

"Peter," Tian lets his name out like a long sigh. "You don't think we're that stupid, do you? We know your restraints are off.

We've fought before, and I'd really prefer to skip that step today if you don't mind."

"Sounds good to me," Peter replies as he brings the cuffs he's been holding behind his back forward, still keeping them in a tight grip. "Loosen my feet and I'll be on my way."

"You know we won't do that. Can't do that, really," Tian continues, making a motion with his hand for his men to make their move. "There are plans already set in motion that need you to be here for the time being. And, fortunately for you, not only alive but also well," Tian concludes as he takes a step closer, keeping one eye on Peter and the other on his men, who are also slowly closing in with extreme caution.

Sizing up the situation, Peter keeps his eyes on the needle, knowing he can take any of these men if needed. The tension on the cuffs begins to make his knuckles white.

"While I do love a good mystery, is that really all you're going to tell me?" Peter asks still holding on to his sarcastic tone. "Must you be so dramatic, Tian?"

"Sometimes a little dramatic flair helps with the distraction," Tian says and gives a quick nod as Peter feels a pinch in the back of his neck. Before he can react, Peter is out cold.

Tian turns and places his empty syringe back in the black box as one of his men comes out from behind Peter with an identical syringe, having injected Peter with a sleeping-serum cocktail to keep him out for a couple of days. Long enough for Tian to get everything else in order. Motioning for his men to take Peter away to the cell they have prepared for him, Tian tries to keep his excitement bottled up. With Mandy home and now Peter officially under his watch, Tian feels his plan falling into place.

The man in the suit returns to the room, passing by Peter's limp body being carried away.

"You're right. He is cunning. But I can tell you know him well enough to contain him your way, for now," the man asserts. Turning to exit, he adds over his shoulder, "We look forward to your reports," letting these words hover as he departs.

Annoyed at the reminder that he still has to report to

others, Tian doesn't let this take away from his victory. Especially since his plan is running so smoothly. Standing alone in the dark room, Tian takes a moment to congratulate himself.

He's one step closer to healing the world.

19

Opening up the door to her new master suite, Mandy sighs a breath of relief in seeing all of her things already unpacked. Framed pictures hang on the walls, various awards sit on her new dresser, and even the bed is made, ready for her to crash out on. The room itself is larger than she imagined. Her favorite part is the set of bay windows next to the bed, complete with a bench filled with pillows where she can look out across The City.

Settling down in the room, Sasha and Mandy both sit on the brightly colored quilt atop the twin bed. Even in this larger room the bed is exactly the same, being just large enough to not fall off of. All Mandy wants to do is sleep for the next week, but she knows Sasha will never stand for that. At least a couple stories will be a must for this evening.

"So, Secret Agent, tell me your tales," Sasha begins, playfully putting her chin in her hands and staring at Mandy.

"You know you can't call me that!" Mandy states getting up to check the door, making sure it's closed tight, then over to the windows to ensure they too are sealed. "You're not even supposed to know where I've been," she continues in a hushed tone.

"Oh, phooey! You know everyone's downstairs eating. Who's gonna hear us up in your ivory tower?" Exchanging looks, Sasha takes it down a notch. "Fine. How has your week been? Meet anyone interesting?" she coos and wiggles her eyebrows, making Mandy giggle a little as she returns to the bed and sits nearest the window.

"I feel like I'm in junior high here," Mandy whispers in an excited tone, feeling her sleepiness slowly fading.

"Right! Don't you love it?" Sasha cheers, bouncing a little

on the bed. Mandy keeps a straight face a moment longer and then breaks, first with a side smile and then breaking into a full-on grin, pulling a pillow to her face and letting out a girlish scream.

"Okay, fine. It is fun to have something more to talk about than our street evangelizing. To go on an actual mission was hands down the most exciting thing that has happened to me, period. And you know I've been around awhile."

"Oh sure, rub it in," Sasha half-jokingly replies, not being a Near Mortal herself.

"Ha! Hey, you asked for it. And besides, you know what they do to people like me, so I don't think rubbing it in is quite fair," Mandy teases.

"No, you're right, the discrimination alone is something I will never fully understand. Sorry. It's just funny fighting for a cause that I will never comprehend completely," Sasha replies and takes a deep breath. Letting it out, she continues with a more playful tone, "Anyways, you're stalling. How *was he*? Was he as smooth as they say? Was he as handsome as they say? Was it scary even?" Mandy leans in closer to Sasha, who returns the motion and comes closer as well.

"I know we've had a lot of secrets in the past, but this is seriously just between us. Never to be shared with even one of our other friends, or even to our superiors. Not even if Ti— I mean, The Director himself if he asks you. You have to keep anything we talk about between you and me." Sasha is taken in by this speech, almost mesmerized by her serious tone and passion. It takes a second for her to answer as she snaps out of her trance.

"Absolutely, Mandy," Sasha states in a serious tone. "I'd never tell a soul our secrets."

Mandy takes out a small pocketknife from her back pocket. Sasha's eyes widen, but she immediately puts out the palm of her hand. Mandy flips it open and moves towards her palm. Sasha closes her eyes in anticipation. A few moments go by until a *thud* makes Sasha jump. Opening her eyes, she first sees the knife sticking straight up out of the nightstand next to Mandy and then Mandy's face as she bursts out with laughter.

"Sasha!" Mandy finally gets out through bouts of giggles. "You don't think I'd actually cut you, do you?"

"Honestly?" Sasha gapes, now laughing a little herself. "You *have* seemed different tonight. I mean, I know we've only just been reunited but, Mandy, you've become one serious chick! I honestly had no idea," she concludes, pretending to wipe sweat from her forehead.

"Well, I love that you were willing," Mandy replies with a warm smile and takes Sasha's hands in hers. "You are either a truly good friend or a crazy person. Either way, I'm grateful." Leaning in, they hug for a moment. "Look, I know you want more, and I promise you'll get everything you're looking for, but tomorrow. I am so tired tonight, I really need to go to sleep, my friend." With a slight look of disappointment, Sasha nods her head.

"I get it. You've been through what I can only imagine is a lot these last twenty-four hours. I'd be able to do more than imagine if *someone* would tell me things..." She pauses and smiles before adding, "I'm joking. Get some sleep. I can hold on to the suspense till breakfast."

"I will say that he is nothing like the stories circulating around about him. Peter was less a ladies' man and more a gentleman." This gets a wide grin from Sasha. "We had a very enjoyable time together," Mandy ends.

"You mean *night* together," Sasha remarks with a smirk, standing up from the bed. Mandy joins her, standing with a slight blush, and they both cross to the door. "I am thrilled your mission went well," Sasha says, embracing Mandy once more. As they release, she adds, "It's good to have you home." Sasha heads down the hallway and back to the elevator, leaving Mandy alone.

Mandy heads directly to bed. She turns off the lamp next to her as she closes her eyes, ready to finally get some rest. Exhausted, but now overly tired, all she can do is think about Peter. His smile, his smell, his hands. These thoughts keep her up for some time and transition into her sleep, providing a wonderful array of dreams.

20

The following morning and the days that follow feel like a waking dream to Tian. His inbox is a symphony of good news, filling up hourly with check-ins confirming Peter is still in his bunk and that Mandy's health is impeccable. Taking a few sips of his morning coffee, Tian opens a couple dozen of these emails, becoming more confident in his plans with each message he reads. The only thing that still gnaws at him is the fact that Peter has not yet attempted to escape or even shown any interest in doing so.

From the moment Tian was first introduced to Peter—the potential *Immortal*—as a target, he knew he would be his key. Having grown up in an overpopulated section of The City himself, Tian learned at an early age that this world is not big enough. Both his mother and father worked multiple jobs to support the alley home he grew up in. Envious of their neighbors just next door in the high-rise apartments, Tian strove to make his life more. To not only move up within his socioeconomic standing but to help his world. To find more space.

When he learned in school about Near Mortals, those that take up Earth's valuable and limited commodities for much longer than any one human deserves, Tian found his calling. Eradication. Then found his focus in Peter, deriving pleasure from the moment he first encountered this being. He would run tests that would bring the legend of immortality to its limits. But Peter never disappointed, always surviving. And to Tian's dissatisfaction, always escaping. Sometimes with the help of an insider, sometimes by pure luck, this man consistently slipped through.

All past encounters began with a minimum of two escape efforts within the length of captivity that they already have held him for this time around. These efforts, of course, ended mainly in Peter's recapture, but this time there has not been even a hint of him working out a plan. Normally this inconsistency would drive Tian crazy. But with things going so smoothly, even Peter's actions, or lack thereof, cannot damper his spirits.

Pushing aside this tiny voice of concern, he focuses on his primary task for the day—scheduling his first on-the-books, face-to-face meeting with Mandy since her return. Brimming with excitement, he stops clicking through his reports and uses his office line to dial the main coordinator.

"Scheduling, this is Lanell," comes a thick, silky voice with a hint of boredom.

"Hello there, Lanell. Tian here," he pipes with a chipper pitch.

"Good afternoon, sir," she replies with a more professional tone. "How are you today?"

"Quite well, Lanell, thank you. And yourself?" he continues, enjoying the rapid change in her demeanor.

"The weather's beautiful and I have a view, so I'm doing great. What can I do you for today, sir?" Lanell continues, nervous to be speaking with someone so high in command.

"I was just checking in on Mandy's schedule. I'm hoping to set up a meeting with her sometime this week. The earlier the better," he answers and begins absentmindedly doodling on the notepad in front of him.

"Well, sir, you do set up her schedule," Lanell answers in a slightly confused tone. "I imagine whenever you'd need to—"

"Now the thing is, Lanell..." Tian cuts in. "I don't want to disrupt anything that's already set into motion," he finishes, wanting to make it clear that Mandy's tests are a top priority. "I'm looking for a time outside of her current tests and other activities that are already set for her."

"Of course, sir," she replies quickly, leaving Tian with a pause and the sound of both the mouse and keyboard clicking simultaneously. She reports as fast as possible, "It looks like, sir, I can set a thirty-minute meeting on Wednesday at 2 p.m. Does that work for you?"

"That it does," Tian replies as he draws a large number two on his sheet of paper and continues to draw around it.

"Great, sir. Is there anything else I can do for you today?" she asks, trying not to sound too scripted.

"That will be all. Thank you for your help, Lanell," Tian answers with a genuine smile on his face.

"You have yourself a good day now," she adds.

"You as well," Tian responds jovially and hangs up the phone.

As he enters this into his appointment book, Tian finds his mind still wandering its way back to Peter. He picks up the phone and dials the head of security but hangs up immediately, not wanting to make a big deal out of this annoying feeling. Switching gears, he instead logs into the security schedule, adjusts the hours allotted, and then shoots the head of the department an email requesting a tighter schedule for the guards assigned to Peter until further notice. Hitting send, Tian immediately feels better. Kicking his feet up on his desk, he stares at the inspirational poster behind him.

"You're right," Tian says to himself. "I *can* do it." He laughs at this, takes a large drink of his coffee, and returns to his inbox.

Not holding his attention long, he drifts back up to the image. The faded Nike Swoosh was something he had learned about in grade school history class. Still feeling a tad anxious about Peter, he picks up a ballpoint pen and goes to begin a brainstorming session about ways to thwart Peter's inevitable escape attempt, but the image on his sheet stops him. While speaking with the main coordinator, Tian hadn't paid any attention to what he'd been absentmindedly doodling. Now staring back up at him is an ink drawing pulled straight from his dreams. A still shot of the underground tomb he so happily stood over just weeks ago during a catnap.

An eerie smile grows on his face as he recognizes this landscape, impressed by his own artistic ability. This scene makes him even more inspired to keep Peter in one place. Flipping over to the next sheet of paper, Tian begins to write, brainstorming ways to catch Peter once he enacts his escape plans. Having played this game of cat and mouse with Peter for so long now, Tian knows that eventually he will get out of his cell. But from there to the outside is a different journey altogether. One that Tian will ensure Peter does not finish.

Needing something a step above creative, Tian writes everything he knows about Peter. He wants to make a lasting impression when they thwart the inevitable escape attempt. He pairs his list with every possible exit and hiding space within the entirety of The Facility. This time, Tian will keep Peter for good.

21

The more security check-ins Peter receives, the more he knows he needs to escape. Even though it's been nearly a decade since they last secured him, Peter still feels that something is off. Something different from any of his previous times spent here.

From day one, Tian has made it clear that there is a pressing need for Peter to be here. Yet, despite all this urgency, Tian hasn't shown his face since. In all the years he's been taken in by this organization, Peter has never gone this long without a visit from Tian, and never without a battery of tests. No tests and no Tian make Peter both nervous and curious at what they have him here for and what is keeping Tian so absent.

Even with escape being on the forefront of his mind, Peter has to give it to them, his accommodations are far superior to even some hotels he's recently stayed in. It's still a cell, complete with triple-locked doors, an inability for Peter to control anything electric—the lights coming and going with the passing of the fictitious day and night—and the usual array of monitoring equipment. All typical cell stuff, and yet he also finds himself in a lovely one-bedroom apartment setup, complete with a stocked refrigerator and an enormous king-size bed. The living room is stocked with an impressive assortment of books, a couple even by Peter's father, on a large bookshelf.

At this point, Peter calculates that he's been down here for about a month, estimating primarily from the light cycles and the guards' shift changes. Being a sociable person at heart, Peter has already befriended most of the guards that make their rounds to his cell. Some stay and chat a bit, occasionally joining him in a cup of tea. Even those that do just the minimum spot check and leave are all very pleasant and, Peter can tell, have zero idea why he is locked up down here.

Working out his escape plan, Peter knows that these guards will be his key out. Having memorized their schedules, Peter has to choose one that he can manipulate just enough to allow himself access to an unlocked front door. From there he knows the layout of this place so well that, no matter where this new cell is located, he is positive he can navigate his way out.

Always game for a brief chat and tea after he's swept through the apartment, Peter knows Hank will be the easiest to take advantage of. Hank never seems to be in a hurry to get to his next checkpoint, and this kind of willingness to be behind schedule is exactly what Peter is looking for. While he hates the idea of hurting someone who is quite lovely to him, Peter also knows that if he doesn't make his move soon, he will find out exactly why Tian is so desperate to keep him down in this luxury suite. And this is something Peter does not want to learn.

22

Mandy knew that pregnancy, especially hers, would come with tests. But she had no idea there would be so many, and so soon into gestation. Of course, this pregnancy is more than just an ordinary one, and The Facility is doing everything in its power to ensure the success of not only the birth but her survival post-partum as well.

The long-standing urban legend that a Near Mortal gains her longevity by absorbing her mother's essence at birth has been haunting Mandy since Tian first approached her with this assignment. While she isn't a superstitious person, it doesn't help that every Near Mortal woman on record has indeed died within hours of giving birth to her offspring.

Shaking this recurring thought off, Mandy reflects on how exhausted she is. While it's only been a month, she already feels like a guinea pig. Desperate for twenty-four hours with no tests, she takes a piece of paper out of the desk drawer and begins drafting a note to Tian. She bluntly states that if she doesn't get a break soon, she honestly isn't sure she'll make it through the next eight months. Knowing she would reword this note before sending it out, her colorful language makes her smile and relieves a bit of built-up tension.

A knock on her door interrupts her writing and slightly startles her. Without getting up, she leans back in her chair and swings the door open.

"Come on in," she says casually as she pivots her chair back towards the desk.

A man enters, dining cart in tow, and begins placing food on the only unoccupied surface in her room—a waist-high dresser. Mandy doesn't look up, completely enveloped in her letter to Tian. As the man finishes, he returns to his cart and begins to leave. This prompts Mandy to at least acknowledge the gentleman.

"Thank you," she expresses, looking up from her writing and giving the lanky gentleman a slight smile.

"Of course, Mandy," he replies and exits the room, closing the door behind him.

His knowledge of her name, while not surprising, still takes her aback, as she does not recognize him at all. Before her assignment, Mandy prided herself in the fact that she knew everyone in The Facility. Yet only weeks after her mission, it seems as if an entirely new crew has come aboard.

Shaking off her surprise, she finishes the first draft of her request letter. Pushing away from the desk, Mandy rolls her chair over to the assortment of breakfast foods. Today she's gone for a more balanced dining experience than usual, opting for a plate of assorted breakfast meats, a stack of fruit, and a pair of waffles.

Oh, do they smell good! Mandy thinks to herself as she lifts the lid. After spreading some butter on the waffles, she continues to stack all the other elements on top until everything is in one tall stack. A waffle, meat, and fruit tower.

Feeling very pleased with her creation, Mandy thinks back for a moment to when she used to take pictures of such masterpieces, sending them out into the vast world of the internet for no one in particular to enjoy. Now she can't even remember the names of those applications, programs she used to use and check hourly. She shakes her head slightly. Things such as social media went out with free speech so long ago, it's hard to recollect.

Grabbing a fork, she digs into her meal and immediately discovers that the fruit is a tad difficult to keep in place. She uses her left hand to balance the forkful on its journey upward. A breakfast like this makes Mandy forget for a moment where she is and what she believes is very likely to happen to her in about eight months.

She has always been known in her social circles as the tough one. Even as a child, she was the first one to stand up for what was right. She suspects this personality trait is the primary reason she made the cut for this assignment. Sure, she's Peter's "type" and more loyal to The Facility than most, but her stick-to-it attitude and her never-back-down reputation led Tian to her in the first place. He'd all but said as much during that fateful meeting in the coffee shop.

That's the thing, she thinks to herself as she finishes up her meal. *I was chosen!* If any Near Mortal woman can survive birth, it will be her. She knows it. Tian obviously knows it. And soon the rest of the world will know it too.

23

Peter sits on his couch expectantly, tea brewing in the kitchen, ready for his security check. The sound of keys comes from the front door, causing various locking mechanisms to release. Peter begins to stand but rethinks this and sits back down, grabbing the book he was reading the night before from the coffee table. It dawns on Peter that he is being filmed, so he tries to look as nonchalant as possible for both the cameras and the incoming guard.

"Hey, Hank. How's it going?" Peter greets the guard, setting his book down and turning around to face Hank, who has now entered the premises.

"Pretty much the same as yesterday," Hank responds with a smile, clipboard in hand. He does a quick scan of the living room and dining area, checking off boxes as his eyes survey the living space.

"Yeah. I hear that," Peter says in his best "bro" voice, his eyes drifting over to the table where the tea is all ready to drink. Trying to seem as natural as possible, Peter walks over to the kitchen table and sits down, motioning for Hank to do the same.

"Aww, thanks Peter, but I've got a lot to do today," he says as he heads straight to the bathroom, only spending a few seconds inspecting it.

"Are you sure?" Peter asks with a longing expression on his face. "It's already brewed and at the perfect temperature," he continues, lifting a cup in Hank's direction. Hank pauses, his face scrunching up in contemplation. "You know how many visitors I get these days," Peter adds, setting the cup down in front of the empty seat across from him. Hank glances at the security camera in the kitchen, then shrugs.

"If it's already brewed, I can stay for a few moments," he replies while sitting down. Taking an initial cautious sip to test for heat followed by a few large gulps, Hank finishes his tea before Peter has even taken a drink of his own.

"You must be in a hurry," Peter remarks, picking his own cup up and taking a sip.

"They just have us on a very tight rotation right now," Hank shares. Then thinking better of it he continues, "But it's nothing I can really share with you. You know, you being the one I'm mainly guarding and all."

The phrase *mainly guarding* sticks out to Peter. Until this moment he's always assumed he is the only prisoner here. But *mainly* implies there are more. While intriguing, right now Peter's goal is to focus on keeping Hank in this cell a little longer. Peter makes a slight humming noise as he slowly takes a sip of his tea, working on drawing it out.

"I have noticed you and the other guards seem much more rushed with your check-ins lately. The others are even less social than before," Peter continues, reaching for the teapot to offer another cup to Hank. Holding up a hand to decline, Hank glances at his watch.

"I am sorry to drink and run, but I really do have other —" A panicked look flashes across his face as his entire body clenches. "If you'll excuse me," Hank grunts, quickly standing up. "I think I'll take a quick detour before heading back out," Hank states with a nervous laugh and heads straight to the bathroom, slamming the door shut behind him.

As expected, the eyedrops didn't take long to kick in. The moment the door slams shut, Peter is on his feet and off to the bedroom. He grabs the supply bag he's packed piece by piece over the last few months and heads to the restroom, lightly knocking on the door.

"You okay in there?" Peter calls out to Hank. Only groans come from the other side, and Peter knows now is his time to move. He opens the door a crack and spies the keys. While Hank is bent over the toilet, Peter grabs them and makes a dash to the front door.

Fumbling with the keys, it takes Peter a moment longer than he'd like to get the correct key in the right lock. Finally unlocking the menagerie of security devices, Peter exits and is deposited into the warehouse.

"Huh," he breathes to himself, slightly surprised that he's been in the middle of the warehouse the entire time. While it has grown tremendously since he last escaped, he still has enough knowledge of the area to determine where the best exit will be.

After more than enough time for Hank to have regained his composure, it surprises Peter that there are no sirens, no flashing lights, not even a guard strolling along. Even with it all seemingly in the clear, Peter knows that something is off. Working on ignoring this feeling, he begins to run, running past exceedingly long storage aisles, past what looks like a row of holding cells, and finally seeing a sign lit up with the word *EXIT* on it.

I suppose even evil underground warehouses need to follow some safety procedures, Peter thinks as he slows down, realizing that running straight to an exit sign might be a little too ballsy, let alone risky. Having just blown his friendship with Hank, this may be his only shot.

Turning down the aisle closest to the sign, he starts to zigzag his way closer to the exit. He still doesn't see or hear a soul, but he is so close now he can taste freedom.

Just one more aisle, Peter thinks as he's about to round that final corner. Taking the last zag, a sudden sound stops him dead in his tracks. Not an alarm or anything that would make him initially think they're alerted to his escape, yet just out of the ordinary enough to give him pause. A buzzing noise coming from the direction he wants to go. Right next to the exit.

Holding still, he hears it again. A click followed by a low buzz, getting louder with each click. It's so familiar and yet such a distant memory he really can't place it. The only thing he knows for sure is that he has to continue forward. Partly because it is the only exit he's aware of, and partly because he's too curious about this mystery noise to turn away.

As he rounds the corner, Peter's brow furrows with confusion. Stacked in front of him is a ten-foot-by-ten-foot wall of old-school, push-button televisions. The clicking and buzzing had been these guys turning on and warming up, and now on each and every screen is Tian's face.

"Peter!" Tian chirps, seemingly looking down at him from this massive blockade.

Peter, frozen in his steps, just stares up at this wall of nostalgia. Tian's face blinks out and in its place is black and white footage of Peter's escape, him leaving the cell, then an aerial shot of him and his zigzagging. None of this really surprises Peter. He knew there were cameras, he'd just hoped to get out before eyes were on them. While disappointed at being caught, he's also impressed with Tian's creativity. Doing a slow clap, Peter comes all the way into the open.

Poor Hank, Peter thinks, realizing that he burnt a precious bridge in vain. He can sense the encroaching guards.

"Tian, you got me. Do you really need to bring in the thugs?" Peter asks, still looking up at the mass of TVs once again displaying Tian's face. A multitude of Tians play across all the screens this time. Tian laughs.

"Not really a need as much as a want, Peter. I don't trust you, and I'm far from being done with you. I consider them insurance." Finishing, he leaves the frame. His image is replaced with that of a bobbing jack-in-the-box head, with its forever-smiling expression and dead eyes looking straight at Peter.

Despite wanting to turn away, Peter keeps his gaze forward. He prefers the image of this doll over facing the thugs that are not so quietly surrounding him, hoping that if he ignores them long enough, he can just get on that elevator and ride it back to freedom.

After only a few moments of watching the bobbing clown head, there is a tap on Peter's right shoulder. Looking to his right, he immediately feels a sharp pain in his jaw followed by a blow to his ribs. Peter collapses to the ground. A guard physically lifts Peter's head as Tian approaches, wearing the same grin as the clown head.

"You think you're so smart," Tian whispers so that only Peter can hear and motions for one of his thugs to lift Peter completely up, allowing Tian to jab Peter in the gut. "But I'm the smart one," Tian finishes with yet another punch that buckles Peter's knees, leaving the thugs as the only thing between Peter standing and falling. "I'm the one that always catches you and then allows you to leave. A little catch and release program, if you will. But this time you won't be so lucky. This time you're mine," Tian says as he cocks his fist back, ready to give another blow.

"Enough, Tian. Enough," Peter squeaks out between gasps. "I get it. I'm the trout, and you're the mighty fisherman. Please, just bring me back to my cell."

Peter looks straight at Tian and meets his eyes. He can see deep rage in them, more rage than one individual has for another. Something more profound that Peter's never understood about this man, nor wanted to.

"That's the thing you don't seem to get here, Peter. You're not the one in control. I say when it's enough!" With that, Tian's fist meets Peter's face. Tian then signals for his men to drop Peter, causing his body to crumple onto the cement floor. Peter watches as Tian's boots and those of his thugs walk away.

Guards arrive as Tian gets into the elevator. Once the doors close and Tian is officially out of sight, they help Peter to his feet and back to his cell, which thanks to Hank—and to be fair, himself—reeks. The guards quickly close and lock the door, leaving Peter alone. He heads straight to the bathroom to check out the damage Hank has inflicted, finding a gigantic mess and a note written on his mirror in what he can only assume is Hank's shit that says, "Thanks for the tea!"

Peter just turns around, letting the door slam behind him, and heads straight to bed, feeling more defeated than he can recall ever feeling in his life.

24

Mandy feels more and more isolated as the weeks fly by. Her only socialization comes from the men who bring her food and the men that take her to and from her tests. The more she thinks about this, the more she can't remember the last time she's seen a woman besides her nurses.

Where are all her friends?

Where is Sasha?

Mandy knows they all are here still, doesn't she?

Either way, she is going stir-crazy.

Mandy throws on the first pair of pants, top, and cap she can find before heading to the door. But just as she grabs the handle there is a knock from the other side.

Startled, she jumps back. She's unsure of whom it could be, seeing as she hasn't ordered any food and her morning tests happened hours ago.

A second knock comes.

"Come in?" Mandy answers, half as a request, half as a question.

The door opens to reveal Tian's beaming face. Mandy, so happy to see a new face, immediately hugs him. Then, remembering he is not only her boss but also the head of this organization, she quickly lets go and backs up a few steps.

"Director!" Mandy says, composing herself. "It is so good to see you."

"Going somewhere?" Tian asks and motions to her cap.

"Oh, this?" Mandy says as she casually removes the cap and tosses it onto her desk. Laughing awkwardly, she stammers, "I was just…"

"Just wanting to get out? To take a stroll?" Tian finishes for her with a grin.

"Kind of, yeah," she replies sheepishly. "Nothing too long. I've just been feeling a little…" Mandy trails off, searching for the right word. "Cramped."

"Well, we can't have you just going out on your own right now," Tian says. At this statement, Mandy's expression gives way to her disappointment. "Look, no need to get down about it," Tian quickly replies to this look, taking a step forward and closing the gap between them. "That's why I've come up here. To take you out. We have a few things to chat about. The second phase of your journey has finally arrived."

Mandy is relieved by the idea of going out but is taken aback by the phrase *second phase*. She doesn't, however, let this show, as she is truly ready to get out of this room. In all honesty, she would take anyone up on the offer to just get out.

Tian motions towards the open door and allows Mandy to exit first. There's not a sound to be heard as they walk down the long hallway towards the elevators, which sends a slight chill up Mandy's back. Until this moment, it never occurred to her that she might be the only one living on the entire floor.

They arrive at the elevators and Tian pushes the down button. He then turns to Mandy with an offset grin, and the same feeling she had when she was in his office returns to her spine as she tries to reciprocate the smile. She's able to force one onto her face just as the elevator doors open. They both enter and stand in silence until the doors open again, letting them out into the front lobby.

Mandy heads straight for the main exit that will allow her access to the outside world. A world she's been craving for weeks now, having only viewed it from her window as of late.

"Mandy," Tian calls out to her with a singsong tone. "This way." He motions to a grouping of potted bamboo plants she has never really given much notice to in all the years she's worked here. Reluctantly, she makes a U-turn and follows Tian towards and then around the plants, surprised to see the narrow hallway this bamboo has been hiding all these years. The hallway leads them to a brightly lit room with an enormous mirror and a tiny elevator. From chills to a stomach drop, Mandy's body rebels at the sight of the mysterious elevator.

Tian pushes the only button on the wall and the elevator doors immediately open. Getting in first, Tian motions for Mandy to join him. Realizing she's come too far to back out now, she obliges and the elevator doors close.

"Don't be nervous, Mandy," Tian says to her as he takes one of her hands into both of his, rubbing the top of it soothingly. "You're about to get a greater understanding of all the work you've been doing."

"Okay," she replies as she gently removes her hand from his. While she's excited at the prospect of this disclosure, there is something in Tian's delivery that makes her take pause. She also just really wants to go outside but can tell that this elevator is for sure going down, a direction she wasn't even aware existed in this building from the ground floor.

The elevator doors finally open, revealing a chasm-like storage space, potentially a warehouse of some kind. Mandy shoots Tian an inquisitive look.

"Come," he insists, hurrying through the warehouse before stopping at a door labeled *This Is Not An Exit*. With a thumbprint ID, he opens the door and holds it wide to allow Mandy passage to his *real* office.

Entering the room, Mandy sits down on the first thing she can find, a couch, and takes a moment to digest what she's just experienced. She rapidly runs off a list in her head.

There is a secret elevator that leads to a sublevel in the building I've called home for nearly a decade.

Tian has a secret lair.

I'm about to be clued in on more than I bargained for.

Scanning her surroundings, Mandy notes that the office itself is sparsely decorated. The room is large but bare, aside from a couple posters tacked up on the walls showing people working together for the greater good, a huge chalkboard, the couch she is currently sitting on, and a desk. Not much else occupies the space. Mandy's chills return instantly as her eyes stop on one poster in particular. The image hanging directly over Tian's desk portrays a giant hand reaching down for what looks like a child's hand. The background is intensely black, and the smaller hand looks like it is reaching out from a cavern as it is entirely enveloped by the surrounding darkness. There is no motivational phrase or saying. Only the image.

"Mandy," Tian says as he takes a seat behind his desk. Mandy startles at her name, quickly blinking away from the image and focusing on Tian's face. Tian notices none of this and continues.

"I know we have already asked so much of you, and you have really delivered spectacularly, from your seduction to your now pending motherhood," he says motioning to her slowly growing stomach. "You have been more than just a great asset to this cause, you are the *poster child* for our entire organization!" Tian pauses for a moment to allow Mandy to soak in his praise.

This phrasing makes Mandy look up at the image above Tian again and brings an uneasy feeling to the pit of her stomach.

"With all that said, your journey's not quite done," Tian declares.

Obviously, Mandy thinks as she absentmindedly touches her belly.

"It's not just the birthing," Tian says, reacting to Mandy's movement. "There's no easy way to say this, so I'm just going to come out with it," he says, now leaning forward. "Peter is here, Mandy."

Shocked by this announcement, Mandy lets out an unintended gasp as her right hand covers her mouth.

"I know this makes no sense to you, but you know how important he is to The Facility, and once we knew where he was..." Tian pauses and stands up. "Well, we couldn't help but pick him up." Tian walks around to the front of his desk, leaning back on the edge facing Mandy. "And this is where you come in, my dear."

Mandy is unsure of what to do with any of this information, and it dawns on her she has no way to know where she is or if anyone else knows. With this thought, she lets her hand slowly drop to her lap and tries to make her face look as open to this information as possible.

"He has already tried to break out, not that he's in a cell or anything as horrific as that. But we need something, or someone, to calm him down. To keep him here until we can fully understand his progeny," Tian says leaning forward, taking both of Mandy's hands into his. She allows this, outwardly appearing fine while inside her head she's screaming. "So, we're going to *capture* you," he declares and drops her hands, which retreat directly to her sides. "This way he'll be protective of you, or of the baby. Either way, once he finds out about the baby, there's no way he'll risk an escape."

Tian walks back to his desk and sits down in his chair. He leans back and places his hands behind his head, looking very proud of himself and this plan. Mandy tries to mimic this emotion, working up a tight smile. But after only a few moments she cracks, finding it hard to hide her emotions even this early on in her pregnancy.

"Honestly Direct—er, Tian, I don't understand why you have him here at all. We're trying to unite the mortal population with Near Mortals. That is the goal. My baby is the potential next step in this genetic leap. How is Peter's presence needed?" She can feel herself getting angrier than intended and takes a slow breath.

"Mandy," Tian says smoothly, leaning forward. "Peter is so much more than just the father of your child. Of course the baby is important, but we need to know so much more about Peter. As the only known Immortal, he may be the key to unlocking the origins of the *Near* gene, understanding why or how he is truly Immortal, and why or how individuals like yourself have such extended life spans," Tian finishes, mentally adding, *and how to put an end to you all.*

"Of course... I get the connection, and the importance of

Peter, but—" Mandy begins but is cut off by Tian before she can finish her thought.

"If we can figure this all out then our cause will be that much closer to having an answer. A solid reason that can finally unite both sides." He takes a quick pause to let this explanation sink in. Pleased she is not trying to interrupt again, he continues. "With Peter here and once your child is born, we can do tests to see just how alike these two really are. We can reach the goal we are all striving for," Tian finishes, raising his hands in a triumphant gesture.

She has to give it to him. Tian knows how to deliver a speech. But while she sincerely wants to be all in, especially with this baby coming, there is something still not sitting quite right with her about his story.

Tian can see in Mandy's expression that more convincing is needed. He stands up and crosses over to his blackboard, picks up a piece of chalk, and begins writing. Mandy leans side to side as she tries to see what Tian is doing, but his back inhibits her view. Moments later Tian makes one last bold stroke with the chalk and turns around, revealing a list of more than a dozen women's names.

"What is this?" Mandy asks as confusion graces her face, pleasing Tian.

"This is a list of all the women that took up the same mission prior to you," Tian states as he watches Mandy's face go from confusion to distress. "I'm sure you've been wondering why we've essentially Rapunzelled you since your return." He glances back at the board. "Each woman was impregnated by Peter, but not a one survived." Tian lets this sink in for Mandy.

This is Mandy's breaking point. She takes a couple deep breaths, trying not to overreact, although she's unsure if any reaction can be an overreaction after everything she's just learned. She knows the lore and is aware that this assignment has the potential to end badly for her. But having such concrete evidence in front of her face creates a panic she's never felt before.

"This is why we're being so careful with you," Tian continues. "Up until this point, all the other women were mortal, as we couldn't find any Near Mortals as brave as you. As we explained during your training, we..." Tian pauses, wanting to make this more personal and hit even closer to home. "*I truly believe that you can withstand this abnormality,*" he finishes and crosses closer to her. "From all the tests we've run, your health is already leagues beyond any of these other women," he says, gesturing towards the blackboard.

Gathering her thoughts, Mandy takes one more breath in and out, trying very hard not to freak out. She chooses to pick out the most pertinent issue and stick to that.

"I already know this pregnancy is a risk," she starts. "What does any of this have to do with you now holding Peter?"

Tian, impressed and surprised by her composure, continues without missing a beat.

"Well," he says slowly. "I am just trying to show you the true side to Peter," he reassures her, trying not to show that he's making it all up. He hadn't expected the conversation to go this way after such a reveal. "I'm sure after the night you had together that you hold a certain perspective. But I assure you, Peter is the womanizer you've been led to believe. He cast away each of these women after one night, and I'm sure would have done the same to you if you'd given him the chance."

Mandy finds all her fantasies about Peter falling to the wayside, now seeing him for what he really is—the *ladies' man* they all had described him as.

"Well shit, Tian," she spurts out without any regard for whom she is addressing. "This information would have been great to get before I went and got knocked up by him!" Mandy, furious now, stands up from the couch and paces.

This is more of the reaction Tian was expecting.

"We knew you were the right one, Mandy," Tian quickly adds, trying to reel her back in. "Believe me. We have learned so much from these past women, and you are nothing like them. You will be fine. We must keep Peter here to ensure that we can not only learn more from his genome, but also so we can compare Peter to his—or rather, *your*—offspring." Mandy stops pacing and stares straight into Tian's eyes.

"And if I refuse? Why would I want to live with this man? A man that has casts away so many other women," she states with a tone filled with disgust and fear. "This is more than just a womanizer. He's..." Mandy can't continue, now lost for words. Tian jumps in, trying to fix this unexpected reaction.

"Mandy, I know these names are a lot to bear the burden of," he says in a low voice and crosses back over to the blackboard, slowly turning it away from them. "And I stand behind the fact that Peter is not a good man. But I've observed him several times, and one thing I know about him is that he protects what's his. Once he knows you're pregnant with his baby, he will protect you," he finishes and goes back to his desk. "And that's exactly what we need, for him to have a reason to stay here. That way we can run tests not just on you and your baby, but to compare this all to his genetic structure as well. It's really the entire point of your mission, to create a child to unite. A child that goes beyond the current genetic makeup of your class and moves us all to a new level," Tian concludes, slightly believing his speech himself, caught up in the moment. Mandy returns to the couch, trying to keep her facial expression nutrual.

"When do I have to make a decision about this move?" she asks without looking up at Tian.

"The sooner the better, but you can have a day or two to think it over," Tian replies. "If you choose to, you can stay in your room and we will continue the tests until your child is born. By that time, Peter will have most likely escaped, so any chance at being able to understand how alike your baby is to him will be much more difficult, if not impossible." Tian crosses over to Mandy and reaches yet again for her hands, but she pulls away. "I get that you're mad. Should we have disclosed this information to you before sending you out on this critical mission? Maybe we should have. But Mandy, this is the most important mission I've ever been in charge of," he pleads, catching her eye and maintaining eye contact. "I knew the moment I heard about you that you were the only one who could pull this off, and I *still* know that to be true."

Looking past Tian, she immediately sees that damn poster. This time she finds herself relating to the tiny hand being enveloped by darkness.

"I'd like to go back to my room now," she murmurs, not looking at Tian.

"Of course," he complies without another word, not wanting the impact of his speech to fade.

They walk hastily through the warehouse, neither saying a word. Both elevator rides are excruciating for Mandy as her mind races. She pictures those last moments on the roof overlooking the Steamline. She needs time outside now more than ever but recognizes it won't be happening any time soon.

When they arrive at her room, Mandy goes straight in. She wants to shut the door on Tian but hesitates, knowing he is still her superior—and really, more than that these days.

"We will give you forty-eight hours to decide, Mandy," Tian says to her, allowing her to then shut him out.

Needing to work all of this out, she goes straight to her desk, takes out a brand-new notebook, and begins freewriting all of her thoughts. Not until every last emotion is out of her head can she even begin to make a rational decision.

Tian stands on the other side of her door for a moment, knowing that he cannot forcibly remove this woman. At least not today. While time is of the essence here, with Peter being more creative than ever in his escape attempts, Mandy isn't going anywhere. There is a reason they chose her—her commitment to this cause is beyond anyone else at The Facility. Combine that with her biological need to protect her offspring and Tian knows she'll come around.

As he heads back to the elevator and then to his mock-office, Tian makes a list in his head of the things he needs to do to ensure that Mandy's final decision on this matter is the correct one. That moving in with Peter is not only her idea but the only option that she can see.

25

All the air fresheners in the world couldn't remove the stank aroma of Hank's bathroom message. Even days later, Peter still notices the occasional whiff of defecation.

"Oh, the smell of defeat," he bemoans to himself, indulging in a serious pity party.

The lengths to which Tian has gone to keep him here in this odd apartment cell causes Peter to worry, even more so after Tian's strange display of dominance with his TV setup. Tian had never gone to such elaborate lengths to thwart Peter's escape attempts in the past. Dwelling on this recent exchange, Peter alternates between anger and confusion, going over his track record of breakouts and confirming that all his previous attempts were successful.

I'm either off my game or Tian's gotten a lot better since our last rumble, Peter thinks as he rolls over in bed. A bed that only adds to his puzzlement. Why is he being held in a pretend apartment? Why isn't he being poked and prodded? Where are the tests? Where is Tian?

A brief knock at the front door followed immediately by a guard letting himself in stops this train of thought. With the ever-changing parade of clipboard-wielding men—never women, he notices—checking every corner of his dwelling, all Peter wants to do is sleep.

Sleep away his defeat.

Sleep away this stupid mock-apartment.

Sleep away Tian!

26

With a deadline of forty-eight hours given from Tian upon her departure, Mandy practically wears a hole in the carpet of her room from pacing back and forth. She needs to work out all the bombshells that Tian dropped on her, alternating between her inability to sit still and bursts of writing. She stops only when her hunger becomes too unbearable. She's thankful that she's not yet in the constant pee stage of pregnancy.

Research has always been her outlet. After her initial decision to go on this mission, Mandy had spent a lot of late nights in careful thought leading up to the big day. If she is completely honest with herself, the motivation of this action had not been entirely selfless. She wanted to make a difference. She wanted to be more than just a cog in a wheel, or some other metaphor she's heard a million times. In the end, the opportunity to be the mother to the greatest asset her cause has ever known was more than she could pass up.

Now faced with the reality of her situation, she's unsure of her next move. Her notes lying out on the desk in front of her are a jumble of past expectations, present realities, and every bit of research she can remember. Not only research from the few days before she made her choice to go down this road, but also everything she knows as fact from all her years working for The Facility. At the forefront of Mandy's mind is the new information regarding Peter's previous seductresses, and how none of them had survived. Even if they had only been mortal, this information seriously scares Mandy and makes her question her decision for the first time. This self-doubt upsets her more than anything Tian can say or do.

A laugh escapes her with the thought that she had propositioned Peter on the train. She'd allowed herself to think *she* was in charge.

He's good, she thinks as she again journals about her options, feeling the forty-eight-hour deadline closing in with each passing moment.

In her heart she is still fiercely loyal to her cause, and with that, loyal to The Facility—the organization that gave meaning to her very existence. She'd covered up her longevity for most of her life before finding The Facility, leaving a long string of unfinished life stories in her wake. Mandy finding this place was more like a spiritual awakening than a job or a career. The institution itself had been founded by Tian, and she'd known about it for nearly twenty years before finding herself ready to stop the cycle of running, finally ready to face who she is. Having come in as an intern, she never would have imagined that she would now be faced with such a complicated choice.

The word *choice* makes her chortle, realizing of course that in the end Tian will have his way. But the thing is, Mandy knows Tian is right. Having Peter here is an important component to understanding the magnitude of her child's longevity. But while she did sign up to carry the baby, it was never part of the deal to also have to live with this stranger, especially after fully understanding his *ladies' man* reputation. She's also slightly embarrassed that she'd fallen for it in the first place, how he pretended to fall all over himself when they began their night together. She has had a hard time not thinking about this man since their encounter, jaded as these thoughts now are from the recent background she's received about him.

Taking a deep breath, Mandy spreads out every sheet she's written on in the last thirty hours: pros-and-cons lists, past and present research, charts on survival rates, and recent demographics of those fighting so hard against her race. All of it adds up to one thing for Mandy. Setting her emotions about Peter aside and taking out her *Mandy The Social Justice Worker* persona, she already knows the answer. This exercise is just a way to talk herself out of it. Yet the reality of the situation is clear. She is still all in.

She is moving in with Peter.

27

Mandy is tough, Tian knows this. Even though keeping Peter here is a high priority of his, the baby's safety is at the top of his list. Thus, Mandy's happiness is up there as well.

Not briefing Mandy on Peter's capture had been a strategic move, partially to keep Mandy from saying no to the idea of seeing the man she was to seduce more than once. But mainly it was because the capture of Peter was never a sure thing. Over the last couple decades he's worked for The Facility, there have been more than a handful of times where Peter slipped through his fingers and then gone into hiding for years. Why set himself up for a nearly impossible conversation if he didn't have to? He would be ready to cross this bridge once they got to it, breaking Mandy down as rapidly as possible. Yet now that he's over the bridge, he isn't sure that he likes the view.

Patience, however, is his strongest virtue. While he will hold Mandy to the forty-eight-hour deadline, if she chooses to stay in her room Tian will just begin a new tactic to change her mind and continue to pivot until she comes around to the correct decision.

Glancing at the monitor installed in his desk, Tian checks in on Peter and finds him still in the same place he was at his last check-in—bed. This makes Tian exorbitantly gleeful, seeing that his impact on Peter is so profound. Leaving the monitor up, he grabs a sheet of paper and writes *Make The Right Decision* on top of it. He writes the first scenario he can think of where Mandy turns down this opportunity to live with her baby daddy, creating an entire dialogue rundown of how each argument will be overcome. This is all in preparation for his next encounter with

Mandy which, looking up to the nearest clock, Tian realizes is almost here.

Enjoying conflict and the drama that can ensue from it, Tian's heart races a little at the prospect of her refusing. Of course, he'd love for this to go smoothly. But convincing someone to do something that they truly, deep down do not want to do? Well, that is his favorite thing.

Halfway through writing his third draft of this conversation, his landline rings.

"Yes?" he answers in a tone that makes it clear that this better be important.

"Mandy reached out to us, sir. She's ready to tell you her decision," the voice of Sergeant Region says. Tian looks at the clock again. There are still a few hours left before the deadline.

"Interesting," Tian replies slowly. "Please let her know I will be up at the deadline."

"Will do," Sergeant Region responds and hangs up.

Unsure how to feel about Mandy's pre-deadline decision, Tian knows one thing for sure. He will not release control of this situation. She will stay on *his* timeline.

With this thought he continues his objection list, feeling that it is more important than ever to prepare for their one-on-one.

28

Patience has never been one of Mandy's virtues. Nonetheless, being told that Tian won't be up in her room until the deadline does not surprise her in the least. She's worked for the man for over seven years now. Even though her personal interactions with him only started recently, she knows he runs a tight ship and already had a feeling that he wouldn't drop everything just to come talk to her.

But that doesn't stop the budding anxiety Mandy is feeling. She wants this to be over already, wishing now that she'd accepted Tian's initial reasoning and moved in with Peter for the good of the baby and to monitor him immediately.

That at least would be an excellent distraction, she thinks while she organizes and reorganizes her notes. She divides her research notes among the pros-and-cons lists, then changes her mind and makes separate stacks for each subcategory. She stops when she realizes that she is no longer organizing but just scattering these pages across her room. Laughing at this, she stacks them all in one pile—no longer caring about the content, just needing them put aside.

Living in this small space and having her only interactions coming from food deliveries and nurses makes Mandy realize that having Peter around will be a welcome change, even if her perspective of him has changed drastically. With her notes already assembled, she continues with this instinct and begins packing. She assumes that once she tells Tian that she's ready to make this move, the move will happen that day. She quickly finds that packing is not the time-wasting activity she'd hoped it would be, as she really doesn't have much to pack.

Frustrated, she crumples up on her bed, ready to give in to the nap that has been pestering her for the last hour. Closing her eyes, she is just about to drift off when a knock comes at the door. Realizing she's lost track of time, she jumps up and opens the door just as Tian prepares for a second knock. He looks from her to the suitcases sitting in the middle of the room.

"Decided I might as well get a jump on packing," she states as coolly as possible off his look, figuring that is as good a way as any to let him know she is indeed ready to leave.

"So, you are moving then?" he asks plainly.

"Yes," she responds, wanting desperately to grab her bags and leave.

"Perfect," he replies, not wanting to say anything else that may change her mind. "I see that you already have your bags packed, and that is wonderful..." Tian trails off and pauses, trying to think exactly how to deliver what comes next. "But you won't be leaving this very moment."

Losing a lot of momentum, Mandy tries not to let her disappointment show on her face.

"That's not to say you're going to wait long. We just need to place you in this new home at the right time. And two o'clock in the afternoon really isn't that time."

"Okay," she says quizzically. "Then when is this *right time*?" she continues, trying not to sound like a petulant teenager.

"Mandy, I'm so happy you're on board," Tian responds, ignoring this attitude, chalking it up to her pregnancy hormones. "I'll be sending up some of my team to prep you on your new living situation so that you won't be going in blind. Then tomorrow, at the break of dawn, you'll begin this next phase," he ends with a grin on his face.

"Sounds like a plan," she responds, not hiding her disappointment in having to stay in this room another night. Before bidding Mandy goodbye, Tian pauses in the doorway.

"What made you change your mind?" he can't help but ask. Looking up at him, she works on quickly changing her demeanor. He is still her boss, and she is far from the sullen child she is currently acting like.

"I gave it a lot of thought," she says as she motions to the loose-leaf stack of papers on her desk. "And you were right. There was a reason that you chose me, and a reason I signed up for this mission in the first place. I can now see the need for Peter in this scenario. After some time to reflect, which I thank you for, I can clearly see your point of view and that the greater good outweighs my potential discomfort."

Impressed and relieved, Tian's smile widens even further.

"That is fantastic to hear," he expresses and turns back towards the door. "I'm truly glad you came around. Although I never doubted you would," he finishes and exits before she can respond.

Mandy falls back on her bed, ready to rest until it's time to move. She's unsure of how to feel about the need to be prepped by Tian's people and still wishes she could go outside. Even though she is going crazy from so little human interaction, she currently finds herself grateful that she has a little more alone time before her new living arrangement begins.

29

Still depressed about his defeat, Peter lies awake in bed and debates getting up—or perhaps even getting dressed—today.

Whatever today means, he thinks, loathing these artificial sunrises and sunsets. Pulling the blankets over his head to block out the synthetic daylight, he chooses to stay in bed until they come and drag him from it.

As he's drifting back to sleep, Peter hears a clinking noise coming from the kitchen. Not aware of any guards entering, his curiosity quickly gets the better of him. Jumping out of bed faster than his sore body likes, he pauses for a moment before pulling on the closest pair of sweatpants he can find and cautiously opening his bedroom door. Peter immediately hears more sounds coming from the kitchen, accompanied by the smell of—he swears—bacon. Peeking around the corner, he sees the familiar silhouette of a woman. As she turns around, plate of pancakes in hand, his eyes widen at the sight of her.

The Wolf.

Despite knowing that Peter lives in this apartment-like cell, the sight of his head popping around the corner gives Mandy a little start. She does her best to not let it show on her face.

"Good morning," she chirps as she sets down the plate of pancakes on the kitchen table, appearing as nonchalant as possible. Peter slowly moves around the corner, stunned with confusion. What is his one-night stand doing in lockup with him, he internally questions as he inches his way into the kitchen. Cautiously grabbing a chair from the table, he pulls it a few feet back and straddles it, never taking his eyes off The Wolf.

"Breakfast?" she offers with a smile as she sits down at the table and begins serving herself. Starving, she couldn't care less if he wanted to eat as she could eat enough for the three of them. Trying her best to be natural, she finds it hard to even manage a fork with him staring at her. But the knowledge that there are enough surveillance cameras to catch anything less than kosher helps her relax and focus on her current passion—eating.

This has to have something to do with Tian, Peter thinks as a slew of questions flood his mind. Is Tian picking up every woman he beds? Is The Facility better at tracking him than he's given them credit for? Had The Wolf been sent to him from the beginning? Why would Tian send him a one-night stand? Spiraling, Peter stops this thought process and scoots over to the dining table. He realizes he's still never had a meal at this table, only an occasional tea when guards would join him, typically preferring the couch and the company of the TV.

They both sit in silence for several uncomfortable beats as Peter watches Mandy eat, Mandy allowing him to do so as she becomes more content with each bite.

"How are you here?" Peter blurts out with unexpected force, figuring the best way to break the silence is to go the direct route and frustrated with this woman's ability to focus so intensely on eating. Mandy looks up at Peter, the direct eye contact sending a bolt straight through the both of them. Putting her fork down, she takes a moment to wipe her mouth and thinks back to the story Tian rehearsed with her. She decides to go with half-fiction and half-honesty, hoping the mix will come off genuine.

"I used to work for the institution that is currently... *housing* you," she states delicately.

"Used to?" he inquires, holding his face still while his head races with even more suspicion.

"Let's say I had a falling out with the guy in charge. Had to take my leave," Mandy explains and pauses for a reaction. Peter gives none, so Mandy continues. "I had quit about a month before meeting you. After committing over seven years of my life to this organization, I needed to travel around awhile and work out what my next move would be. We had our night," she says and motions towards him with her fork, already craving more food. "And then the following morning after leaving you, The Director approached me himself. Apparently, they knew we had been in contact and wanted me to come in to answer some questions."

This makes Peter shift a little in his chair. He knew they kept tabs on him whenever they could, but to take people in for questioning? This is all so bizarre to him. Not wanting The Wolf to observe his inner dialogue and eager to hear more, Peter keeps a straight face and motions for her to continue.

Seeing this reaction, Mandy keeps going down this trail.

"At first I thought it was about them wanting me to come back to work. That is, until your name came up." This statement makes Peter slightly twitch and encourages Mandy even more. "I tried to tell them we hadn't done all that much talking. That's when I realized what they were really after." Mandy takes a bite of her nearly finished pancake, partially for the suspense but mainly for her insatiable appetite.

"Yes?" Peter urges after Mandy goes for her second bite of food.

"Sorry," she says, mouth half-full. "I'm just so hungry these days." She quickly grabs her glass of water and washes the food down. "Okay. Sorry again, didn't mean to leave you with a cliffhanger." Making direct eye contact with him again, she continues, "This is where it gets a little complicated. It seems that you and I were more compatible than we planned that night." Unsure of what that could possibly mean, Peter just continues to stare. Grabbing her water and lifting it to her mouth, she says, "I'm pregnant," and then takes an intentionally long drink.

"Pregnant?" Peter manages to get out, choking on the words. He's flooded with a mix of panic, anger, and confusion. He's already caught her tell—a slight lift of her right eyebrow when she's lying—and has determined that the majority of her story is comprised of fiction. But the pregnancy, that is real. And to Peter that is all that really matters. While he has absolutely zero trust in her, if she is carrying his offspring then the least he can do is be cordial to her. Especially since it seems like they will be sharing a close space, assuming she isn't just here for a visit. Judging from the suitcases in the living room, she is here to stay. One happy, captive family.

Peter realizes he needs to take control of this situation.

"Well, I'll go ahead and shift some things around for you," he says to Mandy as smoothly as possible, still working out a strategy in his head. With that, he stands and heads to the bedroom.

Stunned by his immediate acceptance of her news, Mandy decides to go ahead and roll with it. "That would be great," she replies with a little more enthusiasm than she means to. She compensates by turning her attention quickly back to her meal, finishing her pancake and grabbing one more. Peter turns back towards Mandy.

"It just dawned on me, all I know you as is The Wolf," Peter says, trying to lighten the mood. Mandy explodes with laughter, desperately in need of the release despite knowing the reaction doesn't fit his remark. Gaining control of herself, her gaze softens as she looks up at him.

"Mandy," she replies with a soft smile that makes Peter's heart skip a beat.

"Mandy," Peter repeats back and continues into his room, upset that every fiber of his being is still drawn to this woman.

30

Only a couple months in, Tian already finds himself thrilled with Mandy's performance. Watching their daily interactions with his morning coffee, even from this two-dimensional view he can tell she's already got Peter in the palm of her hand. He knew she was loyal to this work, but it wasn't until he could watch her in action that he could see how great she is. All her little touches, her subtle comments about the baby, even her nostalgic reminiscing about trains. Every bit adds to the deepening of her connection with Peter and to Tian's ability to keep him put. Even though Tian can tell that Peter is leagues away from actually trusting her, there is a beautiful mistrust that Tian revels in.

With a good six months still before them, Tian knows he can let things simmer for a bit and focus on other projects until the birth. But while he has other important things to get to, his thoughts continually circle back to Peter and Mandy. Maybe for the mere reason that he despises Peter and hates that he's getting any enjoyment out of his captivity, or perhaps for his recent realization that he's actually become quite fond of Mandy. Not romantically, but out of respect for her work ethic. His admiration grows more and more with each viewing of the two of them.

Tian knows, as everyone in their society does, that getting pregnant is a death sentence for Near Mortals. The mere fact that Mandy knows this and still went through with the mission makes Mandy that much stronger compared to most people he knows—Near Mortal or not. True, the eradication of her kind is Tian's primary life goal, but he finds himself sincerely hoping that his calculations will be correct. With Peter's loathsome genetic makeup, this child should not need to take Mandy's essence, or however it works. Tian has never believed in the urban legends about why Near Mortal women die, believing instead that their deaths are a part of their disorder. And yet, he also finds that he genuinely believes Mandy will be the first to survive her pregnancy. He can only hope he's right.

However, Tian's thoughts quickly turn from his appreciation of Mandy back to Peter. Since the first moment he caught wind of Peter's existence, Tian knew he needed to find out if *The Immortal* could procreate. Could he produce a human far worse than any Near Mortal would ever be? His efforts to find Peter and begin his test to prove Peter was Immortal ended up propelling him as a leader within his organization and ultimately to founding The Facility.

To the outside observer it seems as if Tian is dedicated to his job, putting in the time and even following up on leads that help multiple Near Mortals on his way to the truth. Of course, these Near Mortals are merely collateral damage as far as Tian's concerned, not meaning to help them at all. But in the end, being at the top of the food chain at The Facility ends up being the key to not only finding but also testing Peter and his unsuitable life span. Humans with longer life spans that still eventually die are bad enough to Tian, but if Immortals begin popping up, well, that will be the end of civilization as far as Tian is concerned.

Sick of looping this in his head, Tian is ready to focus on a different project. He switches his monitor device off and it lowers back into his desk. He turns his attention to his holoscreen and goes through his to-do list as he combines Mandy and Peter's open cases into one larger file and moves them aside with a flick of his wrist accompanied by a sigh of relief, acknowledging that these two people are only a fraction of his master plan.

Sticking with the internal projects of The Facility, he turns his attention to the growing number of captives they have down below. It had originally started as the perfect home for wayward Near Mortal children, the orphans left at hospitals after their mothers passed away from birthing them. Tian, of course, has a hotline for such cases, with moles at every hospital in both The City and The Air City. He's disappointed that he's only been able to amass such a small number of these small Near Mortals—but not surprised. Afterall, most of these afflicted women are able to worm their way into families that support them and that will take in their abominations after birth.

Moles like these are just the beginning of the underground society Tian is a part of. Many of these like-minded individuals are below his pecking order, as he prefers, but a few are still above him. They all share the same goal: wiping out this population of humans whose life spans would create chaos for those that need the room to survive.

Space for those that truly deserve it, Tian thinks to himself.

"Now that's not a bad slogan," Tian muses as he grabs a piece of scratch paper and jots it down. He then reads out loud, "Space for those that truly deserve it," and smiles, setting the paper over in a stack with other slogan ideas, drawing a star on the top right corner.

These thoughts bring him back to his current captives. Raising the monitor back up, Tian clicks it on and again sees that not much has changed. Mandy is finishing up with the dishes in the kitchen and Peter is still in the bedroom. He knows from experience that Peter can be very stubborn and can also sleep like no other. He also knows that Peter has a soft side, and that Mandy is already a part of it. Knowing he really just needs to give them time, he turns the monitor back off.

He realizes that he also needs to provide himself with some time away from them, or at least from Peter, as he tends to become slightly obsessed. Tian leaves his office, carrying with him a feeling of victory. Aware that this is only a small win, he is still happier than he's been in months. Closing and locking his office door, he leaves with a joyfulness that can only be known by those that don't just *work* towards their goals but *achieve* them. And with this piece of the puzzle finally squared away, he knows he will be one of them very soon.

31

As the artificial days pass by, Peter's resistance to Mandy dissolves. The trust might not be there, but her presence still affects him. After what Peter calculates as over a month going by, he realizes they aren't going to take her away anytime soon. Mandy being there also raises Peter's uncertainty about what Tian is up to. What could the endgame be? Are they just supposed to become a happy, captured family living out their days underground, their child never knowing what the sky is like, or fresh air?

The idea makes Peter furious. He knows that getting both himself and Mandy out will be hard, yet easier now than with a child in tow.

That thought still throws him.

Child.

A child.

His child.

Peter had never even given thought to reproducing, having lived for centuries producing no children thus far. His feelings towards fatherhood still up in the air, Peter fortunately has an excellent distraction—planning their escape.

The family thing can wait until we're free, he figures as he puts the final touches on his plan.

The one thing he never counted on is having to *convince* Mandy to leave. Although she claims that she's worried about the baby, there seems to be something more underneath her reasoning that Peter can't quite put his finger on. It's true that she has several clinic visits a week and it could simply be her survival instinct he is picking up on. But whatever it is holding her back, Peter knows he must break through it, and fast.

Playing a few angles with her, he begins with the cramped living space, then to Tian as an evil overlord, and finally breaks headway with the idea of raising their child underground.

"You make a good point, Peter," Mandy states while eating her second breakfast. "This *situation*," she says while making quotes, "is not really the best environment for the baby in the end." She pauses to take a large drink of orange juice. "If we're going to get out of here, we should do it while I can still maneuver," she continues while rubbing her now five-month-pregnant belly.

"I was hoping you would say that," Peter replies, making sure to give as many cameras as possible a bad shot of his face and turning on the blender. Moving right next to Mandy, he whispers loudly into her ear, "I have everything mapped out and ready. We can leave as early as tomorrow morning." Mandy takes another drink of her juice and meets eyes with Peter.

"That soon?" she replies back into his ear, then leans back to look him again in the face. Peter nods. There is a long pause before she turns back to him and says plainly, "Alright," and goes back to eating. On the outside Mandy appears to be calm about this decision, as if she's agreeing to take a stroll after a meal. But inside she's frantic.

How can I stop this plan? she thinks to herself. *I'm here literally to keep Peter in place. And now I'm going along with an exit plan?* Mandy keeps her calm expression and gives Peter a smile before getting up from the dining table and heading to the bedroom. She'll pretend to take a nap while she's actually brainstorming ideas to thwart this escape plan and once and for all give her the leverage she needs to keep them both here through the remainder of her pregnancy.

Stunned by Mandy's change of heart, Peter takes the win and moves forward. He's more than ready to get out before Tian becomes less distracted and starts showing even more interest in him and his growing family.

32

In his underground office—and really, in The Facility as a whole—Tian is king. There is no one higher than him. And Tian loves every minute of this. Yet when it comes to his cause and the Anti-Near Society, there are still some that hold more power than him. People he has to answer to. Has to report to. He is sure that it is only a matter of time before he will be the head honcho there as well, but currently he has to fall in line and do as he's told. Today is no exception, as Tian has his monthly progress report due on his case study of Peter, which now includes research on Mandy as well.

The Anti-Near Society formed shortly after plans to build The Air City began. It was clear to a select grouping of individuals that even by creating more living space via sky expansion that they would still run out of room to live. Things felt dire to those truly paying attention, unsure how much time they had before the human race would run out of room to live. The same organization of scientists and engineers that had plotted out the infrastructure of the planet's livable space were now tasked with expansions they had no room for.

Then the first Near Mortal came out from hiding.

She had been a film actor longer than anyone could remember. No one had really noticed her lack of aging because that's what actors do—they stay youthful. When she made her announcement, others began coming forward with the same symptom and the emergence of an entire subrace of humans came to be. The fact that this new breed, as they thought of them, could live for centuries or longer without dying was just too much for this collective of forward thinkers. Even though every one of these individuals were women and therefore had their own kind of population control, the kind of longevity that these people were speaking about was just too much. And as with most differences in the human race, like-minded people started to find each other.

A few years into Tian's membership, he approached the executive team and pitched his idea for The Facility. *A place for Near Mortals to feel safe.* An organization to stand up for this subsect of humanity.

"What better way to track your enemy than by building their refuge?" he had pitched. Not only did upper management love his idea, but for showing such initiative Tian ended up being put in charge of the entire project.

Glancing at the monitor and seeing Mandy and Peter going through their breakfast routine, all Tian can see are *things* who've outlasted their stay. Sure, on the outside they look like a young couple in love, but Tian knows better. He knows they both have had plenty of time already. Time to make their families, to find that someone. For all he knows, they both have many times over, allowing those that they *loved* to pass away while they continued onward.

Continued to the next love.

Next life.

A life that Tian has yet to sample. Work being his, as it turns out, one true love.

Turning away with a look of disgust, Tian finds any fondness for Mandy vanishing. Retrieving his notes from the inbox, he leaves this office to go upstairs to the conference room, awaiting the weekly call with his superiors.

33

With the escape plan running on a loop in his head, Peter finds sleep elusive, and by the time 2 a.m. rolls around he's more than ready to go. He's reviewed each variation of the plan, this time prepared for any obstacles they may run into and even more prepared for whatever games Tian has planned.

Wanting to give Mandy as much sleep as possible, he wakes her at 2:30 a.m., hands her the tightest clothes she can fit in, and waits as she gathers a few remaining essentials.

Mandy's emotions are in a tizzy as Peter wakes her. She had hoped that he would just sleep through the night, and in the morning they would revisit this escape of his and move on to staying put and waiting for the baby to arrive. Begrudgingly getting out of bed, she takes a quick detour to the bathroom, pretending to go to the restroom but really giving herself a pep talk in the mirror.

"You can do this. You can stop his escape plan and make this right again," she whispers to herself and flushes the toilet to cement her bathroom deception.

Peter motions for her to go to the walk-in closet as she exits the bathroom and sees that there now is a homemade ladder made of their second set of sheets, leading to a hole in the ceiling. A hole Peter only just created about twenty minutes before she awoke. Mandy does not question it and ascends the ladder up into the crawl space with Peter directly behind her, dragging a knapsack full of items. He whispers directions to her as she leads them through a maze of twists and turns in what appears to be the air ventilation system.

Peter is relieved at how compliant Mandy is being with his

directions. He had been afraid she would be more resistant after all the convincing he had to do, but her lack of discussion now makes him feel even more secure in their budding relationship.

Although she is going along with Peter's directions, Mandy is rapidly trying to figure out how to thwart this escape. About to look back and check how close behind her Peter is, she feels something *clunk* beneath her. Immediately frozen in shock, she then attempts to scurry away from her position. Her efforts are in vain as the metal surface she tries to remove herself from gives way. Peter reaches for her a moment too late, leaving Mandy gripping onto the side of the ventilation shaft, the tubing dangling with her in it, inviting her to slide on down. Desperately wanting to pull her up, Peter knows it's much safer to lower her down instead.

"Go ahead and slide down," Peter whispers to Mandy. "The floor is very close to you already," he continues. Mandy does as he directs, landing on her feet.

"Peter!" Mandy whispers desperately with a bit of terror in her voice. "You will not believe what I'm seeing!" she continues, not in the least bit rattled by the near fall, instead focusing on what she's viewing. As Peter slowly lowers himself to the ground as well, all Mandy can do is look at this small room full of children.

The age range seems to be between a few months to five or six years old, with one girl in her early teens. Looking down the line of beds and hardly able to process exactly what is going on, Mandy does a quick count and comes up with ten children in total, all fast asleep. Mandy notes how it is reminiscent of an orphanage from a film with all these twin beds lined up. She remembers hearing cries from time to time echoing through the warehouse while going to and from her tests, but at the time she had passed it off as some kind of auditory hallucination from being pregnant. She never imagined there could be children actually *in* The Facility.

They both stand in silence for a moment. With Mandy still in shock, Peter quickly devises an alternative plan. Escape, at least tonight, is no longer in the cards.

Remembering time is not on their side, Peter quickly snaps out of the shock of the situation before them and inspects the fallen piece of tubing. Since the alarms haven't sounded off, Peter knows whoever is on duty hasn't seen them yet. If they're too busy to catch them live, he hopes whoever reviews the surveillance tapes won't bother to check the footage for this room. Regardless, the tubing has to at least *look* like it hasn't been broken.

Tapping Mandy on the shoulder, he motions to the tubing and mimes that he needs to lift her up to secure it back into place. She nods and they both hand-walk the tube up as high as they can. Mandy, noting that the tubing is quite light, gets on Peter's shoulders and is able to secure the metal back into place. Once back on the ground, Mandy is again transfixed by the sight of all these children.

"Mandy," Peter whispers to no response. "Mandy!" he says again with a little more urgency, lightly touching her shoulder. She turns to him briefly, then back to the children.

"They're all girls," Mandy manages to get out.

Peter just nods.

"You know what this is?" Mandy asks without looking back at Peter, whose face shows that he does indeed, putting together the fact that he is often taken in for testing and that Near Mortals are all women—or in this case, girls. They both know immediately that this is a nest of guinea pigs. Small, adorable, human guinea pigs.

"We have to go," Peter says gently. Turning back to Peter, Mandy's face is full of emotion—not just confusion anymore, but also that of fear and accusation.

"Did you know about this? Did you lead me here on purpose?"

Peter, confused beyond belief, scrambles to deny the allegation.

"Mandy," he begins, trying to stay calm. "I have nothing to do with this organization. They captured me. This is as much of a surprise to me as you," he finishes, trying not to let his immense need for them to leave come across in his voice as insincerity.

Mandy looks back towards the slumbering children—babies, really—and then to Peter. It only takes a moment, but she feels her allegiance immediately change sides. She's no longer able to pretend that The Facility is working towards the good of her people. Knowing Peter is right, that they need to leave immediately, Mandy turns away from the children and gives her full attention to Peter. The stakes are higher now. It's no longer just about the birth of her baby or potentially creating a new step forward in the evolution of humanity. It's also about *them*—these tiny children. If she and Peter get caught this evening, she can never free them.

Having Mandy's full attention back, Peter takes her by the hand. If there is one thing he knows, it is how to navigate this building. They quickly leave through the entry door to the children's barracks and sprint back to their apartment cell. Peter is impressed that Mandy can move as quickly as she does as they zig and zag their way back to their cell just in time for the early morning check. Seeing the guard with his attention enveloped in a broadcast on his ocular implant, they know that timing will be crucial, but sneaking in will not be impossible.

As the guard opens the front door, Peter and Mandy round the corner. Peter catches the door before it can completely latch, giving it a beat before he peeks his head in. He checks to see if the coast is clear, sees the guard enter the bathroom, and motions for Mandy to follow him. Slightly afraid but now running strictly on adrenaline, she follows Peter, allowing him to grab her by the hand as they quickly tiptoe-run into the bedroom. Jumping into bed, they push the pillows that had been lying in their place off the left side of the bed nearest the wall and assume their positions, looking exactly like the pillow lumps moments earlier. Hearing the bedroom door open and close, they know they've made it past the in-person guard. Both lie completely still, waiting for a call to come in from surveillance to expose them. Moments later they hear the front door close, and they know they're in the clear.

While waiting for the front door to close, Mandy feels a rush like none she's ever experienced. For the moment, her thoughts of those poor children leave her head as the adrenaline continues to surge through her body. Without a word, Mandy kisses Peter. She allows the excitement of the moment to take her away, giving into the feeling that has been growing inside her with this forced living arrangement, realizing with each returned kiss she is beginning to care deeply for this man.

It's their first physical interaction since the train, and Peter does not fight it. Aware of the cameras in the bedroom and not in the mood to give the guards on duty too good of a show, Mandy only removes the essentials. Peter does not fight this either, feeling as much excitement as Mandy but for an entirely different reason.

34

The first few days after their escape attempt are silent. They've both been cautious, afraid that they had been caught and Tian is just toying with them, ready to drop in and separate the couple at any moment. But after three artificial day cycles with nothing out of the ordinary, they begin to relax a little.

Mandy now finds herself in full-on planning mode, committed to an entirely new mission beyond herself, even beyond her own child. After stumbling upon all the children in what they delicately refer to as *the orphanage*, Mandy knows she can no longer spy for The Facility and is now stuck with a slew of questions flying through her head.

Is there anything I can believe from what Tian told me?
How safe will I be with this delivery?
Did Peter really discard all those women?
How can we free all those poor children?
What is Tian's real endgame here?
And the biggest question of them all.
Was the plan ever to unite the two factions of humanity?

Peter also has his own doubts, but not about Tian. Tian has locked him up so many times that seeing a dark cell full of kids, while terrifying, is par for the course as far as Peter is concerned. Mandy is who really consumes his thoughts. He's known from the moment she gave her backstory when first appearing in this apartment cell that she is working with Tian in some form or another. He hopes now that Mandy has seen just one atrocity Tian is capable of that she will realize she has aligned herself with the wrong side.

While a part of Peter knows that Mandy has been lying

since the moment she walked into his life, there is still trust there that he can't shake. A belief that she is in this current situation with him for the right reasons, reasons that he would probably get behind if she would just let him in on them. When dealing with Tian and anyone working alongside him, Peter's default mode is to trust no one. Yet all he wants right now is to know if the mother of his child can truly be on his side, but he is unsure of how to access this information.

Sitting in the living room area, they both look up from the books they're pretending to read and catch one another's eye. A quick smile crosses both their faces and they promptly return to their *reading.*

Bouncing from her new distrust of Tian to her growing trust of Peter, Mandy knows she needs to find out who exactly it is that she's living with. Even if she can't trust herself as a good judge of character, she has to size Peter up. Is he the man she met that evening on the train, or the monster Tian has portrayed him to be? But she'll need a private space for this discussion. Mandy brainstorms ways she and Peter can hold a private con-versation in their cell. She visualizes every nook and cranny of their tiny home, trying to find the space for this important talk —one she hopes Peter is also thinking about.

35

Even with all the success he is having in keeping the happy couple together, Tian still receives constant pushback from his superiors and must explain repeatedly how important Peter is. That figuring out what the biological difference is between Peter and Near Mortals can bring them leagues closer to the cure they've been searching for. Not to mention that being able to study the first child of an Immortal could bring them decades further in their research.

But none of this matters to the executive team not onsite at The Facility, who prefer to focus more on the migration pattern of Near Mortals rather than Tian's ongoing research. To Tian's chagrin, none more than Joe. The current president of the Anti-Near Society consistently makes Tian defend his ideas, more so than ever since seeing Peter in person during his last visit to The Facility.

"Besides, isn't that the entire point of all those kids you have down there?" Joe countered at the last meeting Tian was present for. "To find this mutation in their DNA?"

Tian had to agree that this was true. Learning more about this disease is the primary reason they have their collection of mini-Near Mortals.

"We have gathered such significant information from these subjects," Tian had agreed, trying to gain footing in front of his peers. "From calculating the average growth rate of a Near Mortal to understanding the inner workings of their immune system, these little ladies have been a tremendous help. But none of them have the longevity of our *white whale*. I still firmly believe that Peter, and now his offspring, will be the key to putting an end to this contamination once and for all," he concluded with passion to their unenthused silence. There would be little support for the continuation of his project going forward once the child is born. Even when unveiling the fact that this child is going to be male, something that no other Near Mortal has ever been, the group seemed unimpressed.

Frustrated that his vision for where they need to go rarely matches up with the goals of the rest of the board of directors, Tian has stopped attending these weekly phone meetings. He now receives their pushback via email instead. Sifting through a few of these emails currently, Tian shoves down his resentment and returns to the daily reports on the Near Mortal children. Relieved that Mandy and Peter are still behaving, he can actually focus on topics not revolving around them. His attention shifts to his other in-house ventures.

Going over the first few reports about the girls' most recent tests, Tian finds his thoughts immediately drifting back to Mandy. Already past the halfway mark of her pregnancy, in just a few short months they'll begin integrating the newest child.

A boy will be a big change of pace, Tian thinks as he brings up the monitor for Mandy and Peter's cell. With this child not only being male but potentially Immortal, Tian finds it nearly impossible to focus on anything else.

He once again turns his attention away from the flow of emails regarding the Near Mortal children and back to the surveillance of Mandy and Peter. Tian is comforted by the knowledge that soon his attention won't be so divided. Once the child is born, he can focus strictly on *all* the children at his disposal, leaving the two creators to fade away in the deep depths of his Facility.

36

Mandy awakes the next morning with a solution, her dreams inspiring the best place for her and Peter to have a private conversation. Hearing Peter begin to wake up, Mandy leans over.

"Come to the bathroom with me," she whispers into his ear, kissing him on the cheek for show before getting out of bed. She looks back at him with a *follow me* expression before exiting the bedroom.

Confused but very intrigued, Peter does as he's told and follows Mandy into the bathroom where she already has the shower running.

"We need to talk," Mandy says low enough that she hopes the mics won't pick up her voice over the rushing water. She then begins to undress.

Peter immediately gets what's going on. The shower will be the only safe place to talk without prying eyes or ears. He takes this as a good sign, that Mandy may indeed be on his side now, as he too undresses and joins her in the shower.

"This is the only place I could think of where we can have a private conversation," she says the moment Peter steps in and slides the shower door closed.

"This is brilliant," he returns, willing himself to keep his eyes up. Mandy jumps right to the point, knowing that whatever guard is surveilling them will get suspicious quickly with them both out of sight.

"Peter, I know you know that I'm basically a spy. I was planted down here to keep you appeased until the baby comes."

Peter can't believe she's confessing this to him and remains quiet, wanting to hear what else she has to say first.

"I've worked for this cause for quite a few years now and truly believed we were making a difference," she continues before pausing, searching for the best way to explain herself. "But after seeing all those children, I don't know what to think any longer." Becoming unexpectedly emotional, Mandy begins to cry, taking both of them by surprise. Peter goes to hold her, but she backs away, pulling herself together. "Sorry, I'm just a little overwhelmed," she states, wiping her eyes.

"Of course you are," Peter interjects, no longer holding any suspicion for Mandy and letting himself finally and completely connect with her. "I imagine these last few days have felt like you've had your entire identity taken from you. And I am sorry for that. But I'm honestly not sorry you saw what you saw because now you finally understand what kind of organization Tian runs, what kind of man Tian is, and that us escaping before the baby comes is imperative," he responds as quietly as his passion about this subject will allow.

Mandy takes a moment to process Peter's reaction, feeling more and more sure that she can truly trust him. She looks down at her hands and sees that they are already pruning, signaling their time is up. Peter looks at his hands as well and thinks the same thing.

"I hope this leaves us on the same page trust-wise," Peter whispers as he opens the shower door and steps out. Remembering that the cameras can now see him again, Peter leans in for a kiss that Mandy more than happily returns. He then grabs a towel and heads to the bedroom to dry off and dress, leaving Mandy alone with her thoughts.

Staying in the shower, an array of mixed emotions come down on Mandy: mourning over the loss of her organization, excitement about her growing feelings for Peter, and anger towards her now former mentor. She finds the anger building inside of her towards Tian the strongest of the three. She knows that this will be her primary fuel to propel her plans forward—to not only escape with Peter, but also to figure out a way to take every last child with them.

37

Morning Activity Report: Project Love Birds

8:14 a.m. – Subjects enter bathroom together. Observed then entering shower together. Subjects remain out of view for 17 minutes before Male Subject reemerges. Female Subject follows out 2 minutes later.

8:33 a.m. – Subjects resume normal morning routine. Nothing else to report at this time.

– Sergeant Region

When Tian first reads the report from his second-in-command, he chalks up the recent development to experimental behavior mixed with a little boredom. But, as these showers become more of a regular habit, Tian realizes he's lost Mandy.

Despite knowing it had been a long shot to begin with that she would remain true to the cause while literally living with the enemy, Tian still had hoped. Even in his latest briefing with his superiors, Tian had praised Mandy for her impeccable performance around Peter and just how well the operation was going. He had to boast, knowing that there is a strong possibility of getting kicked off the board if his plan fails.

Peter has always been a major distraction for Tian, and now with Mandy and a baby in the picture he finds himself once again pouring far too much time into this subsection of a bigger picture. One that has a slightly different ending than the one he's pitched to the organization. *His* ideal ending. For Anti-Near the ending is quarantine, while in Tian's world the ending will be eradication of the entire species.

Tian minimizes his email window to eliminate the distraction and turns his attention back to his other children, who are all thriving in their Anti-Near training. Tian had developed the training himself to create a hoard of Near Mortals that hate their own kind. Once old enough, they will be able to infiltrate the enemy's world and take them all down from the inside, just like The Facility is set up to do. Like all the Near Mortal organizations are ready to do.

Tian is tired of waiting for the world to catch on and see that there's no room in their civilization for these people. Once the timing is right for the Anti-Near Society to strike, Tian knows the rest of the world will gather behind them, all in agreement that this illness must end.

He continues to work out the logistics of the big event, the ins and outs of establishing these ladies into the right Near Mortal communities to make the impact they need to. Getting his momentum flowing, Tian can feel his passion for the project returning. Meeting with Joe always puts Tian in a bad mood, causing him to doubt his position in the organization. But all he needs to do is look at all the work he does here in *his* Facility and Tian's self-assuredness returns. And he's ready to give these child-shaped bombs the attention they deserve as well.

38

As the months pass, Mandy and Peter become a couple in every sense of the word.

Each morning they perform their breakfast waltz. Peter makes eggs while Mandy pops in the toast, pours juice and milk, and fully sets the table. Following directly after breakfast cleanup is their lunch cha-cha with Mandy leading this time, creating a marvelously light meal from anything left over from dinner the night before, Peter assisting by setting the table and cleaning as Mandy prances around the kitchen being creative. After a few hours break where they read and clean a little around the apartment cell, they begin the dinner tango. Peter leads this one, recreating menus from memory while Mandy acts as his sous-chef, prepping everything needed. Both collapse in the living room as soon as the dishes are done, together and ready to fall asleep and begin again in the morning.

This becomes their routine. And in turn their life. Every meal is eaten together and set up immaculately. Food acts as their distraction, a routine that allows them to maintain their sanity.

Three times a week a new Facility guard takes Mandy away for a few hours, returning her with a little less blood each time. They initially assume these tests have to do with the baby and Mandy's healthy delivery, but with nothing ever reported to them they both begin to wonder what the real reason is behind the multitude of visits.

But each morning Mandy and Peter can feel just how active the baby is becoming, kicking and turning more with each passing day. They both forget for a moment the situation they are in, enveloped by the growing love they find for each other and the child growing within her. When not eating, Mandy spends most of her time with her hands on her belly, cooing to the life that has begun to make itself known. All that Mandy knows is that she will not allow this life to be taken from her, and she's sure that Peter is on the same page. Both try to force out of their heads the likelihood of Mandy's demise, believing that Peter's *difference* will be the key to her survival. A key Mandy hopes to bring to a new generation of Near Mortals.

39

Tian finds himself excited for his monthly visit with his group of youthful Near Mortals. He finds sorting through the weekly reports just doesn't do justice to his comprehension of these wonderful pieces to the quandary that is this disease.

Entering the room they all live in, Tian is greeted with a fullhearted, "Good morning, sir." All their faces are plastered with smiles. Even though none seem sincere, Tian prefers it this way, knowing he has full control of each of these little wonders. Snapping his fingers twice, each child stands at the end of her bed with her arms at her sides, staring straight ahead. Tian then strolls down the aisle, looking down at each little girl as he passes before meeting up with their caretaker at the end.

"They all seem to be in splendid health," Tian comments.

"Yes," she replies with a smile, also far from sincere.

"Can any of you tell your Uncle Tian your favorite memory since his last visit?" Tian asks of the entire group. Each raises and waves a hand, eager to take part. Tian points to the eldest, a tall girl just entering her teens. She turns her body to face Tian before speaking.

"My favorite memory since your last visit was when a butterfly snuck into our room and flew around for over an hour before moving on," she states. Most girls give one clap in response to this tale, agreeing that this is also their favorite memory.

"That is an exciting tale," Tian responds with enthusiasm. The eldest girl turns back to face the center again. "Anyone else?" he asks as he looks upon the group. A tiny girl just shy of five slowly raises her hand. "Yes?"

"My favorite memory since your last visit was..." the girl begins but pauses, beginning to fidget with the hem of her shirt. "Was when we set the butterfly free," she ends with a huge grin, looking from Tian to her caretaker. Seeing neither return her smile, she quickly turns back to center, now looking down at the ground. All the other girls do the same, staring now at their feet. Tian summons a tight smile to his face.

"Well, I can see how that would be a memorable experience for all of you," he proclaims to the room. Turning to the caretaker and speaking at a volume only she can hear, he says, "A moment outside, please." He then announces back out to the room, "This was a very enlightening visit, my dear children." Tian continues talking as he makes his way to the exit, the caretaker following close behind. "I look forward to hearing about more of your *adventures*, but I have some urgent matters to attend to." He turns to look once more at the cowering audience, none daring to look anywhere but down. Not wanting to ruin this moment, Tian opens the door and escorts the caretaker out before closing it behind them both. The caretaker resembles the children in her stance.

"It's not what it sounds like," the caretaker begins. "I only allowed the children to let the insect go in the large apothecary out in the warehouse. They never went outside," she explains before pausing for a moment, her long black hair making it impossible for Tian to view her face. "If that's what you were thinking," she whimpers.

"First off, please look at me while you speak," Tian says, more out of wanting to continue controlling this woman than needing to see her face. She complies and tilts her head up, revealing an expression Tian can tell is supposed to be fear, but lying just beneath is hate. He revels in both.

"You know very well that these children are not to know anything about the outside world until they are fully grown adults. We must maintain control of their environment in order to study them properly. I understand something like an insect getting in is an unavoidable occurrence, but to allow them to interact with it, catch it, and—as they put it—*set it free*?" Tian raises his voice. "If they think the butterfly was set free, then what does that make them?" He pauses, but only for effect, which she knows and makes no attempt to answer. "Prisoners," he states. "And what do prisoners do?" There's another pause as she does not try to answer, only continuing to stare. "Try to free themselves. And the last thing we want is for any of these children to feel like they need to be free from us." With that, Tian is finished.

"I understand," the caretaker replies. Knowing that any kind of argument will be met with another long speech, she adds, "I won't make this mistake again."

"See that you don't," he snaps, then turns and walks away.

She takes a moment to place a warm smile on her face before she reenters the children's room, reeling them back in and maintaining the captive environment. Internally, however, she's mapping out a plan to create the freedom these young ladies deserve.

40

Mandy begins implementing her escape plan a couple days after the discovery of *the orphanage.* The shock of seeing those poor children locked up was all she needed to formulate a plan to break herself out before the baby's due date. She focuses on getting herself free and then, once out and to an Air Colony, she can regroup and return for the girls.

Having worked for nearly a decade at The Facility before being drafted to her current assignment, Mandy's connections run deep. While it takes some time to figure out how to get a message upstairs where her allies are, the effort seems to pan out. Of course, no one she's seen since the moment she started living down here are remotely familiar to her, but Mandy knows more than people. She knows this culture. She knows how to befriend people that are drawn to *her cause.*

She chats up guards and the cleaning crew, hitting one dead end and then another until one night around midnight, while she is having yet another snack, Mandy chats up the right sanitation worker who knows her friend Mal. Mal is the most social person Mandy knows. If anyone would befriend a member of the cleaning crew, it would be her.

It takes three weeks of talking before Mandy finally convinces the young janitor to take a message up to Mal. She writes a message on a napkin while in the shower that morning, stating that she and Peter need relocation ASAP. Mandy folds it up and tucks it away, only discarding it in the kitchen that evening during yet another midnight snack, making sure her new acquaintance sees her motion as she does so. The young man is talented at playing it cool, and Mandy is pretty proud of her budding plan as he leaves for the evening.

It takes two weeks to get a reply, long enough for Mandy to give up hope and resign herself to being in this prison much longer than she could have ever imagined. She's been moodier than normal after her weekly tests, now having to be wheeled to and from her clinic visits via wheelchair due to how weak she becomes after they take her blood. She pays no attention to the guard currently pushing her back to her cage when she becomes suddenly aware of how close the guard's face is to hers.

"Plans are being made," the guard breathes in her ear before straightening back up and continuing to step in rhythm. Those four words liberate Mandy and lighten her as she realizing her friends are indeed out there and her plan is already in action. Mandy knows it will be only a short time before she will be out.

We will be out, she corrects herself. Of course, she plans to include Peter. After all, he is the father of her child, and if things go badly for her at the end of this pregnancy, she already knows that Peter will be there for their baby.

Mandy keeps these plans from Peter, however, not wanting him to stop planning another escape himself. This seems to keep his mind occupied enough for him to remain calm while trapped in their cell.

The very next week at her doctor's visit, she's handed a folder by one of the nurses. As she sits down in her wheelchair, Mandy looks up at her in confusion, having received no information from any of her previous visits. Returning her look, the nurse leans down close to Mandy's ear.

"These are the plans for your last few weeks," she whispers and stands back up, facing Mandy with a straight face. Mandy's face goes from confused to a polite smile, not wanting to give anything away.

"Thank you," Mandy replies with as little inflection as possible. "I've been hoping to get a little more clarification." She clutches onto the envelope almost to the point of white knuckles.

As soon as the guard drops her off at home, she grabs Peter

and they both head straight to the shower. Peter begins to disrobe but notices Mandy is standing in the bathtub fully clothed, so he steps in as Mandy already begins to rip open an envelope he's never seen. A mix of joy and excitement graces Mandy's face, and she brings the document far enough out for Peter to read as well.

The baby kicks. Hand to belly, she begins to hum as a smile crosses her face. She looks up, catching Peter's stare. Neither say a thing as they both know they now have the key to their freedom.

A million questions race through Peter's head, but none seem important. All he wants to do in this moment is place his hand next to hers upon her belly and feel the excitement within. The entire family. Ready to leave.

41

Tian finds himself in a better mood than he can ever remember being in, even whistling while he begins his morning email check-in. He's delighted by the news that Mandy is still keeping Peter in check, which admittedly makes Tian wonder slightly where her allegiance lies these days. But even with the handful of long showers they've been taking, Tian chooses not to worry. He figures that any chance of escape has long passed since the baby is so close to being born.

Tian shares the baby's growth and related reports with all his superiors and finds his clout within the Anti-Near Society seem to grow as well. While it had satisfied him being a big fish in this small pond, a pond he had really built for himself, he is more than ready to move on. He's prepared to move up not only in rank and standing but also in the literal sense, finally getting himself to The Air City and off The Mainland.

Only a couple of weeks out from the child being born, Tian finds himself utterly relaxed. As always, his feet are up on his desk and his monitors are on, but Tian finds today that they're not really showing anything of interest. Looking up at his clock and then back at the monitors, he realizes he can actually shove off early for once.

And why not? he thinks to himself. *Might as well take advantage of this brief window where everything is going perfectly.* With this realization he stands up from his desk, grabs his keys and murse, and heads home for the evening. He hums as he exits the building, a wide grin on his face.

42

The night of the escape starts off like most other nights for Peter and Mandy. The lights in their windows transition from mock-day to mock-night, with tonight's lighting featuring what they assume to be a full moon, creating a brighter than usual blue glow behind the drapes. Peter always laughs to himself about the fact that The Facility goes to such trouble creating an elaborate lighting scheme for a prison cell.

They've been much quieter around each other over the past few weeks, ensuring that no slipups occur when the plan finally goes into effect. With very few words spoken even at dinner time, Peter pushes his food around on his plate, finding his appetite gone as it always is when he's about to do something risky.

"I'm not feeling great," he states to Mandy and to whoever is on night surveillance that evening. "Just leave the dishes for me to do in the morning," Peter continues as he gets up and pushes his chair in.

"No, that's fine," Mandy replies with genuine concern in her voice, empathy being one of her strongest suits. "We can handle these few dishes," she says with a smile, rubbing her hand on her belly to reference their upcoming little helper.

This brief moment makes Peter chuckle a little and fall even more in love with her. Wanting to stay, to take her in his arms and kiss her, Peter knows that right now he needs to go to bed. He has to get as much rest as possible before their connections come through and they find themselves on the run. There will be plenty of time for romance once they are rid of this place. Without another word, he turns and leaves.

Finishing up her meal, Mandy takes care of the few dishes and puts together a little plate of leftovers for herself, then retires to the living area. She clicks through all the nature channels they have access to and comes to a stop on a show about penguins. The baby is as animated as usual, almost kicking the plate of food Mandy set on her extended tummy to the floor. Catching it just in time, she places it on the arm of the couch instead of her table of a stomach and settles back in for an evening with her web-footed friends.

Just as the first episode is coming to an end, Mandy hears a peculiar noise coming from the front door. Looking over, she sees nothing. But as the sound continues this doesn't put her at ease. She gets up and draws near as the sound of metal scraping comes once again in an almost Morse code pattern. Though Mandy knows Morse code, and this is not that. Inching closer to the door, she realizes what is causing the sound and moves just as the door gets lifted off its hinges.

She's aghast at the sight of a familiar face from months ago. It's Elysabeth, her upstairs nurse, who appears in the doorway with one of the main guards. Mandy is speechless. Realizing they must have taken the door off so the guard wouldn't have to use his key card for entry, she shakes off the shock of their entrance, understanding time is of the essence.

Dying to ask why this nurse is helping them now, Mandy instead heads to the bedroom, whispering back to her rescuers, "I'll just get Peter and we'll be off."

Opening the bedroom door, she goes over to Peter to find that he has fallen asleep, having assumed it would be another night of them not being rescued. Before Mandy can finish whispering, "It's time," he is out of bed and grabbing their go bag. They both quickly exit back out to the living room where the guard is waiting with open arms, ready to give Mandy any assistance she needs.

"This is literally your last chance, Mandy," Elysabeth says. "You will be going into planned labor by week's end if you get caught." Mandy is struck with an even stronger sense of urgency.

"Then what are we waiting for?" she responds. She begins pushing forward faster than her legs or belly will permit, using the guard's help to his full capacity. Peter follows directly behind them. Elysabeth keeps pace while prepping a blood pressure gauge, wanting to get one last reading from Mandy to ensure it is safe for her to travel. They tuck themselves into a doorway so the nurse can finish her checkup.

"Is this really the time for that?" Mandy snaps.

"This is the only time, Mandy. Now stand still for ten seconds, won't you?" Elysabeth snaps right back. Mandy complies, and both Peter and the guard keep watch.

These ten seconds feel more like an eternity, the pressure of knowing that any moment Tian may catch them weighs down on them like an elephant's foot. But at the count of ten, the nurse is done. Mandy's final checkup shows she's in excellent condition, and Elysabeth gives the green light to let her go. Mandy laughs at this.

As if they could stop me, she thinks.

"We have more help for you around the corner," Elysabeth whispers to Mandy and Peter. "And more upstairs to ensure enough of a distraction for you two to slip away." Without another word, Elysabeth and the guard retreat into the hallway.

Realizing they've already stuck their necks out far enough for her and Peter, Mandy puts one hand in the air and waves in appreciation, both of them happy knowing that their baby will be fine throughout this journey. With one less thing to worry about, they can now focus on the task at hand—getting out of The Facility.

43

The sizzle of his perfectly seared steak brings a smile to Tian's face as he places it next to the fresh assortment of vegetables he picked up on his way home. Looking them over, he sees deep greens, vibrant purples, and bright reds. Unsure exactly what the mix contains, it excites him to try it as he rarely has time for more than a frozen meal these days. Plate in one hand and utensils in the other, Tian makes his way to the living room where he has the last season of the classic show *Dexter* to watch. Pressing play, he laughs as the opening credits resemble his plate, the first cut into his rare piece of meat causing a stream of blood to merge with his fresh veggies.

Just as he lifts this delectable bite to his mouth, the Red Alert goes off, signaled by an almost comical siren dropping from the dining room ceiling in the form of a flashing red light. Tian calmly places this bite back on his plate, stands up, and walks over to the dining room. He grabs a broom and swings the handle at the light, smashing it and sending shards of plastic flying everywhere. He allows himself this moment of relief from his rage, as there is only one reason his team would send such a message.

They're escaping.

He leaves his dinner and quickly makes his way to the garage. He taps his left temple and dials up his second-in-command. Tian doesn't give him a chance to say hello.

"What the hell is going on?!" Tian screams as he gets into the fastest of the three cars he owns. Normally he'd have to drive his beater to keep up the appearance of being the director of a nonprofit, but tonight he knows he is going to need speed.

"Hello, sir," Sergeant Region stammers from the other end of the call.

"Well?" Tian cuts in impatiently. "I don't want *hellos*, I want answers! Why, during my time at home, am I being interrupted by a flashing red light?!" Pulling himself quickly together, Sergeant Region continues.

"It seems that during the last guard check to the bunkers below, there was no one there to check up on... sir." He adds the *sir* with slight hesitation, filling the void that hangs on the other end of the line.

Tian takes a moment to let this information sink in, racing through yellow lights and trying to will himself to already be back at The Facility. He takes a few breaths in through his nose and out through his mouth, trying to calm down enough to speak again.

"When you say no one there, you mean..." Tian gets out, already aware of the answer he's about to receive.

"That the subjects have escaped, sir," Sergeant Region states as plainly as possible. "At least from their bunker," he adds, hoping to gain a little favor.

There is another long moment of silence as Tian's brain kicks into overdrive, going over every possible escape route they can take. Regaining a sense of power with each slow breath, he quickly comes up with a plan.

"Alright," Tian says slowly and calmly. "I'm about ten minutes away. I want you to get guards at every elevator, especially the hidden ones. And two at every exit out of the building."

"Already done, sir," Sergeant Region replies quickly.

"I don't care if it's done!" Tian snaps, not appreciating the interruption. "Just make sure that it is *really done!*" Tian shouts, then takes another deep breath to regain his composure. "I want you, Sergeant, to physically go and check every exit and elevator in the entire complex."

"Yes, sir," he barks.

There is yet another long pause.

"Now!" Tian exclaims, hitting his steering wheel with the

palm of his hand.

"Right!" Sergeant Region responds, sounding flustered and disconnecting the call.

Tian is unsure if his second-in-command will do what he's requested and begins making a list in his head of replacements for once this crisis is over. This helps him remain calm as he rapidly closes in on The Facility. He already has a good idea of where they're headed, Tian just wants to be there when they once again catch Peter, and this time Mandy. He needs to see their defeat in person.

44

Peter and Mandy make their way through the warehouse quietly, finding that several of the guards are working to ensure their safe passage. More than halfway to the rendezvous point, the entire warehouse is suddenly flooded with lights and sirens, signaling to Mandy and Peter that the guard on duty has found their empty cell. Both realize that all bets are off in terms of receiving further assistance.

Sure enough, the next guard they see doesn't stop to greet them.

"I'm so sorry, Mandy, but we can't take you any further," the young gentleman says over his shoulder as he keeps walking past them, trying to at least throw off their location for the time being. Mandy folds the remainder of the plan that was in her folder and places it in her back pocket. Looking over to Peter, she can see he's already devising a Plan B.

Quickly running through every in and out he is aware of, Peter meets Mandy's eyes. He realizes they need more than just a plan but also the will to continue forward. Looking down the corridor one more time, Peter turns back to Mandy.

"I've broken out of this place more times than you can count, babe," he asserts with a goofy smile and a wink, trying to lighten up both their moods. This makes Mandy smile and relax a bit. "Here," he whispers, guiding her towards an unfinished gap in the wall that leads to a crawlspace between what seems like two sections of the warehouse.

Mandy follows Peter in as they move swiftly in the dark, slinking their way through this hidden hallway. They are spit out near a service elevator that has been inactive since Mandy first started at The Facility. She goes to tell Peter this, but he's already hit the call button, which immediately lights up.

45

"The elevator, sir," is the first thing Tian hears as he enters the building.

"What about it? Didn't you shut all elevators off immediately after getting the alert?" Tian demands from his second-in-command.

"Yes, sir. All *working* elevators," Sergeant Region quickly replies. Tian knows exactly what this means.

The service elevator.

He also knows that this would be a far too simple a way to capture them. There is zero chance Peter would be that sloppy. Not willing to risk it, however, Tian sends Sergeant Region and two additional men over to the elevator's exit, not able to even look at his second-in-command. He takes five men himself and heads to the stairwell near the same elevator.

"How did they get out of their bunk?" Tian addresses the well-dressed man to his left.

"Our current theory is inside help, sir," replies the man. "The cameras were on a looped feedback, so we had no way of knowing the prisoners were gone until the physical check-in." This confirms Tian's suspicion that Mandy has indeed turned on him. He'll find out why soon enough. Making it down to the basement floor, Tian flings the door open.

"Olly olly oxen free!" he shouts and then motions for his men to spread out. Tian heads over to the service elevator, hoping they would leave some tracks as he receives a transmission on his headset that the elevator is empty.

A good distraction, he muses. But as the word *empty* passes through his head, Tian knows precisely where they are.

46

As soon as they see Tian, they know they have to act fast. They stand a strong chance of escaping if they can just get outside. As they watch him walk away towards the service elevator, they take their shot, leaving the passageway between the walls and silently running to the staircase. Peter has Mandy enter first, thinking she will be slower with the baby on board, but she ends up leaving him in her dust and having to wait on him.

The last thing they want to do is open this door to the unknown waiting for them. But it is also the only thing they can do. Staying glued to the wall, they slowly slink in, relieved to see no one in sight. Mandy makes eye contact with Peter and they telepathically debate if they should run for the front doors or not, motioning only with their eyes.

Mandy is then distracted by a light. Squinting to get a better look, she realizes it's not a light—or at least not the direct source—but the reflection of light bouncing off a small compact mirror. Looking even closer, she can see the person holding this mirror is Sasha. Tears of joy flood her eyes at the sight of her dear friend. Grabbing Peter by the hand, they make a run for it.

As they reach her at the exit, Sasha grabs Mandy by the hand and turns to Peter, a conflicted expression on her face.

"I'm so sorry," Sasha breathes as she jabs a taser in his ribs, dropping him to the ground. Mandy, with a look of horror on her face, tries to drop down and assist Peter but is dragged out the exit by her best friend and two others she doesn't recognize.

Peter hardly has time to react, trying to catch his breath.

"Mandy!" he barely gets out before she vanishes down the front stairs. Working on getting up, he makes it to his knees before he's once again bombarded with light. Light and the one voice he hates above all else.

"The double back? Really, Peter?" comes Tian's voice.

Peter cringes at this sound, not looking away from the exit he was mere seconds from reaching. Tian orders two men to go after her, and hearing this Peter knows now it is not Tian's people who plucked Mandy away, and thus they will never find her. This makes his recapture slightly bearable. Tian can see this insignificant victory written all over Peter's face.

"Just because we don't have her now doesn't mean we won't have her soon," Tian says as he approaches Peter. But Peter can see on Tian's face that this is a bluff. Not only does Tian have no idea how they got out, but he also has no idea where Mandy has gone. Up to standing now, Peter turns and faces Tian.

"Alright, Tian. You got me," Peter says with a smirk. "Again," he adds, putting his wrists together as if to be cuffed.

"Oh, we've got you, alright. And no more little luxury suite either. It's full-on medieval dungeon time for you. You know, like it was when you were *young*," Tian says, trying to hide his extreme disappointment at Mandy's escape. Snapping his fingers, they take Peter away just as the men he sent after Mandy return to the lobby empty-handed. Even with Peter remaining in captivity, this massive setback in losing the one thing that truly matters—the child—begins sinking in for Tian.

"Go find Sergeant Region and make sure he knows Peter is secure. Have him come to me as soon as everyone is back on task," Tian commands with immediate obedience. As these men head back downstairs, Tian goes to his upstairs office, the closest place he can be alone. He needs to regroup and figure out not only how this happened but also how to regain control. Control he desperately needs.

47

Mandy is a swirl of confusion as she is pulled by the arm towards the exit and then immediately placed into an Air Cab. They are careening through the air before Mandy can protest against leaving Peter. Peering down, she watches as Sasha rushes back into The Facility, but she sees no sign of Peter. She wants to yell at the cabbie to stop, to turn around, to do something to get her back to Peter, but she knows that it will do no good. Now at an elevation higher than they allow any of The City's traffic routes to go, she knows they are heading to the safe house, the Air Colony Mandy has planned to go to all along. The only difference is Peter isn't with her. She realizes all she can do now is sit, try to relax, and trust that this Air Cab is taking her and her child somewhere safe.

Hours pass. The only thing Mandy can tell is that they are still going up and north as she watches the Northern Star out the driver's side window. She's never been this high before, and even with her guilt over leaving Peter behind still weighing on her, she can't deny that she is enjoying this mode of transportation more than she normally would. From the astounding views to the amazing air system in the Air Cab—equipped with an oxygen modification that makes it so she'll never enjoy the simple act of breathing quite so much ever again—Mandy finds it hard to do anything but relax.

As the sky begins to lighten, Mandy can see the outline of the Air Colony she's headed for. Still nervous about what is happening to Peter, she's also slightly excited to finally reach this Air Colony. These subcolonies are something Mandy's always been fascinated with, created by people who basically jailbroke the technology of The Air City and developed platforms away from the primary structure to make separate towns of their own. Nearing one now, Mandy notes that these masses look like scattered islands in the sky.

Coming in for a landing in this remote air structure, Mandy squeezes the side of her seat at the sight of the smallest docking station she's ever seen. Nearing the landing strip, she can see there is a mass of people gathered all looking up at her cab. Butterflies enter her stomach at the idea of such attention when all she wants to do right now is eat and then sleep, exhausted from the night's activities. After the Air Cab smoothly lands, Mandy thanks the driver and then stumbles her way out of the door, finding herself a little wobbly from sitting so long. A woman with shoulder-length dreadlocks breaks away from the crowd and comes to Mandy's side, helping her regain her balance.

"We are so happy you made it here in time, Mandy," an older woman with striking white hair says as she joins Mandy and her new friend. They both lead her towards the crowd of people. "So happy," says the older woman, patting Mandy's hands. The crowd parts as they walk through and Mandy scans the crowd, hoping Peter has also escaped and somehow made it here before her. After a moment of not recognizing a soul, she turns to the two women.

"You seem to know me, so do you also know Peter?" she asks the pair. "I'm assuming since you got me out, you would have got him as well?" The woman who patted Mandy's hand now grabs it and the other answers in a low and serious tone.

"I'm sorry, but it came down to freeing you or him. And, well, *you* were the priority," she says as she motions not to Mandy but towards her ever-expanding waistline. "Peter was unfortunately recaptured. In the end, this capture was the distraction we needed to liberate you. We had to trade one for the other, you see."

Mandy opens her mouth to argue but lets out a sharp cry and doubles over in pain instead.

"We did indeed get you here just in time!" the white-haired woman says, motioning to two women from the crowd. These women each take Mandy by the arm and lower her down into a wheelchair brought over by a third observer. Moving quickly, they take Mandy directly to a building that from the outside looks like a small cottage but inside holds a surprising amount of high tech. An entire medical staff is standing by and prepped when Mandy reaches a bed.

"Mandy," a woman in surgical gear says softly to Mandy, who is currently gritting her teeth, wishing that all the tests she'd gone through at The Facility had also come with at least a couple birthing courses. "My name is Doctor Genner. I know all about your condition and am completely prepared to bring your child into this world and keep you alive in the process."

Mandy is slightly set at ease with this statement, relieved that they are ready for her birth. Propped up on the elevated bed, surrounded by strangers, and in more pain than she's ever been in, Mandy wishes she recognized even one face in this entire colony.

Popping up next to her bed, Mandy's happy to see the semifamiliar face of the white-haired woman who greeted her at arrival.

"I'm Fran, and here's my hand," she declares and pries her hand directly into Mandy's. "I'm not as fragile as I look, so squeeze hard! You're gonna need to," Fran finishes as Mandy lets out a scream and without thinking does as Fran requests, squeezing harder than she intends and grateful to have someone to hold on to.

The primary doctor positioned between her legs barks orders.

Hold. Push. Breathe.

Mandy follows her directions without question, and after what she is told later was a short period of time, Mandy feels relief and hears the sound she's been eager for since this venture first began—the sharp cry of an infant.

Mandy, excited to meet her child, is shocked with the

speed in which the surrounding masked women carry her baby away rather than towards her. She wants to shout out, but a more urgent need for sleep falls over her, and Mandy is out before they even exit the room with her newborn.

48

Fortunately for Peter, dealing with long expanses of time is something he's become an expert at. Normally he'd have stopped counting days or paying attention to the passage of time altogether, but right now he needs to keep track. With Mandy so close to her due date, he wants to make sure he has a relative idea of when his child enters the world.

No longer living the life of luxury he had in the last apartment cell, Peter now finds himself in a dungeon-style setting —complete with zero windows, one rusty metal door, cement walls and flooring, and a bucket to relieve himself in. To maintain any semblance of time, he resigns to scratching small tally marks on his cell wall every third guard visit, assuming they are giving him three meals a day.

A week into his captivity, by Peter's count, Tian stops by and offers Peter a cigar as he enters the room. Peter declines, not wanting anything from Tian. Remaining stoic on the outside, inside Peter sighs in relief as he takes the offer to mean his child's been born.

"A boy no less," Tian comments as he lights his cigar. "Ten fingers, ten toes. Very impressive. And from what we know—and believe me, Peter, we've looked into this—you and your son are now the only two *male humans* with this longevity disease. But, of course, we're hoping he doesn't take after his dear ol' dad and go full-blown Immortal on us. Near Mortal is bad enough."

Tian stops and just watches Peter for a moment, hoping to get at least a single emotion out of him. Something. Peter doesn't budge, but his lack of sarcasm is enough to let Tian know he's gotten to him.

"You've got to be proud, Peter. Having another male out there to propagate this gene?" Tian jabs at Peter to no avail. "No comment here, huh?" Tian continues and takes a long drag of his cigar. Peter remains in his corner.

Tian blows out some smoke rings, thoroughly enjoying himself.

"It's true our spies have only received this information through the grapevine, to use an old turn of phrase. But it's only a matter of time before I track down your little family and bring them home to you," Tian delivers with a grin that turns Peter's stomach.

There's a succession of three light taps on the door.

"Oh! That's for me," Tian states, putting the cigar out on the wall and placing the remainder in his breast pocket. "Thanks to you and your—or should I say *our*—little double crosser, I've become busier than ever," Tian gloats towards the door. "Figure I'll raise the little tyke as my own. Best way to monitor his longevity."

This gets a slight twitch out of Peter.

"Show him the plague that is your kind. Might even make him a crusader." Tian gives the door four quick raps and it opens a sliver. Peter doesn't budge.

Tian laughs to himself.

"Don't worry though, I'll leave Mandy down here with you. You two can live happily ever after in a cell made for, well, one."

At this Peter is on his feet and lands an uppercut to Tian's jaw before he can react, causing the guards to throw open the door and hold Peter back.

Tian laughs again. This time the laugh is more out of surprise, although still very antagonistic. Peter wants to yell a million different things at Tian, all revolving around the same line of leaving his family alone. But he knows the more of a rise he shows Tian, the more Tian wins, and thus he remains still in the hold of the two guards. Tian turns and stares squarely into Peter's eyes.

"At least I now know that my plan is a good one," he says smugly. Going against his better instincts, Peter tries to lunge forward, to break loose and land one more punch, but the guards are too strong. Tian turns and walks out, leaving Peter with the two monstrously large men, who begin doing to Peter what he would have liked to do to Tian.

Once he's reduced to a heap in the corner of the cell, the thugs finally leave Peter alone. After a few moments of stillness, Peter is able to move his head and glances at the tallies on the wall. He lets out a ragged sigh of relief that Mandy actually survived the process. Both his son and love are alive. A tear rolls down his cheek as he closes his eyes, drifting off to the happiest sleep he's had since their separation.

49

It takes a couple of days, but once everyone is sure that both mother and child are healthy, Mandy and her baby are reunited. She takes her child into her arms, never having believed she could have such a moment. Mandy nearly breaks down in tears, but she knows they will take her little bundle away if she sobs. So instead she coos, singing softly to her child as she had during pregnancy. Looking into the beautiful face of her baby, Mandy realizes she has no idea if it's a girl or a boy. Taking a quick peek, Mandy gasps at the sight of the little baby boy she now holds. A grin that only a proud mother can have appears on her face as the weight of the importance this child carries slowly settles in. Her boy represents the next evolutionary leap for her entire race. Looking around the room, Mandy can tell she is not the only one that knows the importance of this child.

Goosebumps rise as this thought crosses her mind, followed immediately by another. A name. The perfect name, she realizes as the baby stirs a little, stretching his brand-new extremities. A name that comes from a book she grew up with, both her and his father's favorite.

"Hey, little Max," she whispers to him, leaning down and nuzzling his soft cheek. "I have a story for you. A story about your ancestors. One I will raise you on, and once you are old enough, we will change the ending." The baby just looks up at his mom, being very still, seemingly soothed by the sound of her voice.

Mandy remains bedridden the remainder of the week after delivery, appreciating beyond words the hospitality shown to her from these people she's never met. More often than not, her new friend Fran is the one to bring Max in and out for feedings, allowing Mandy to get as much rest as possible. While more tired than she's ever been, she is grateful to be alive. This on its own is a miracle.

It'll only be a matter of time before I truly find out what repercussions having a child will take on me, she thinks while lying in bed by herself, beginning to go down a rabbit hole. *Will I start aging? Is my Near Mortal status compromised, passed on to my offspring? As the saying goes, only time will tell.* She ends on this note. Unable to write any of this down and get it out of her head, she realizes this kind of thought process will only lead to a full-on panic attack.

As the week in bed ends, she is more than ready to get up and start planning. While she's thrilled to be a mother, Mandy finds her mind is occupied with loose ends. She knows she cannot enjoy her time with Max until she ties them off. She must save not only her child's father, but all of those tiny children as well.

I'll return as soon as Max is old enough to be without me, Mandy thinks as she takes Max into her arms, thrilled to be able to do such at her own whim. Strolling around the Air Colony, she makes plans in her head, knowing it will take time to pull off the feat she's about to attempt.

50

Light.

Peter's confident he can feel the warmth of its luminescence as it abruptly pours through the barred opening on his cell door. The medieval-looking door features three thick metal bars, covered in rust and just large enough for one to peer in or out of. Of course, this feeling of warmth is only his imagination. This light brings no heat with it, only a pale white with a slightly blue hue, and a flicker of fluorescent.

The light coming on signals Peter's feeding time.

Peter begins to feel the duration between the guard's visits lengthening, his waste bucket filling up more between pickups. Taking no chances, Tian always has three people deliver the food ration and change the bucket out—one for each duty and one to just stand and, Peter assumes, look intimidating. Which he does.

The Starer, as Peter dubs him, is about a foot taller than the other two and always stands with his arms crossed and a scowl on his face. Peter knows if he is ever to escape that he needs this man on his side. How to win over this statue of a man becomes Peter's new distraction. He fills his time envisioning various scenarios, icebreakers, and ways to let this man see he's not the monster Tian has portrayed him to be. Peter begins with some simple one-sided conversations about past employment and relationships, but he receives zero acknowledgment from the man-giant.

After a few more visits he begins to get a reaction from the other two guards. While the men assigned to these two positions rotate from time to time, Peter soon gets the rhythm down and becomes, as much as he can, friends with each of them. He finds it easy to pick up the individualized conversations and to continue with each recurring visit.

After fourteen visits—discreetly tallied in the corner of his cell—Peter begins gearing most of his comments towards The Starer, at first cracking jokes about his size.

"I'm surprised I never see the dolly you use to bring him down here," Peter quips to a laughing audience of two guards and one straight-faced giant.

A couple cycles through the guard rotation the jokes become more frequent, with some guards even pitching in jokes of their own. One more week of this and Peter finally sees a slight reaction from The Starer. It begins with an eye roll and then a purse of the lips. Peter knows he's getting somewhere and is excited to be moving in any direction.

Then the visits stop.

51

"He's been on one form of formula or another for months now. He'll be fine without me for a couple weeks," Mandy contends exasperatedly as she finishes changing Max's diaper. "Won't you be fine?" she says in a singsong voice as she lifts him up and twirls him around in her arms. "Of course I'll miss him, but the sooner I leave the sooner I can reunite our family." This she says directly to Fran, maintaining her cool tone for the baby's sake as she lays Max down on the changing table to dress him.

"I understand, but your presence on this mission really is not necessar—" Fran starts but is cut off by Mandy.

"I know you seem to think that, but I'm the only one up here who has lived in The Facility, both above and below ground, and the only one who has firsthand knowledge of where the children are located," Mandy says, beginning to lose her cool.

Fran opens her mouth in protest, but Mandy continues.

"And yes, I know that we have many good people on the inside. I'm positive we do. I mean, it's why I'm here today, right? And that is going to help a lot when we all arrive," she argues, tired of going around in circles with her friend.

The baby babbles as Mandy pulls a shirt over his face. Mandy switches back to her baby voice, her focus directed back at Max.

"Yes, it will help a lot," she says more to the baby than Fran. "But Mommy knows the most when it comes to the layout, so Mommy needs to take a quick little trip down to The Mainland to get Daddy and all the young children out of that mean ol' Facility." She picks Max up and swings him around a couple times, then holds him out to Fran. Reciprocating the gesture,

Fran holds out her arms to accept the baby.

"Fine," she sighs. "Just keep in mind that only *one* of you is Immortal and this child would be much better off with two parents rather than one."

52

Only a matter of time...

These are the words written in bold letters on the only poster hanging in Tian's underground office. Normally this phrase would give him strength and reassurance in his goals. Whenever he'd read those words, he'd know that things would all come to be with enough time. But with Peter now under his control, all he can think when he looks at the poster is that eventually Peter will escape. He always escapes.

Banging his fist on his desk, Tian stands and stares at his poster, trying to get the thought of Peter out of his head.

"But he didn't escape, did he?" Tian practically shouts to himself. "He was caught. And not just this time, but on his last attempt as well," Tian assures himself as he paces around his office. "For the time being, you must trust that you can keep him here. The child is your only concern." With that thought, his intercom buzzes and a female voice comes through.

"Sir, the car is ready for departure." Tian walks back to his desk and presses the illuminated button, preferring wired communication to wireless as it's proven to be much more secure.

"I'll be right there," he replies and releases the button. Turning back to the poster with a slight grin on his face, Tian says out loud, "Only a matter of time indeed." He glances at the monitor showing Peter's cell, observing that his bucket is getting full but not quite full enough to need attention.

He picks up his office phone and dials 1-5-1.

"Good evening, sir," a youthful male voice comes over the line.

"Evening," Tian responds. "I'm about to head out. Just

wanted to leave instructions for the Priority One guest. At this moment, one more week will be fine before there needs to be any attention given."

"Yes, sir," the voice on the other end affirms.

"And be sure to contact me if there are any major changes. Beyond that, you can just leave the updates in the online report." Before the desk worker can respond, Tian hangs up. He then grabs his murse and exits his office, making his way to the first floor and then out to the Air Car, ready to find the child.

53

With one last kiss on the forehead Mandy turns away, leaving Max in the very capable hands of Fran.

Very capable hands, she thinks as she hurries away, wiping the tears that form in her eyes with her slightly baggy sleeve.

"Two weeks maximum. Peter and the children. Two weeks maximum. Peter and the children," she chants to herself. Approaching her team, she takes it down from a whisper to a mere movement of her lips.

She doesn't realize she'd stopped breathing until she arrives at the Air Car. Mandy takes in a deep breath. Tossing her bag into the back seat, she climbs in after it and buckles up. She's acutely aware of her two companions looking at her, the driver in the rearview mirror and her second-in-command for this mission fully turned around.

"I'm fine, really," Mandy says to them both, somehow feeling calmer just hearing these words out loud. They both continue to look at her. "Let's go already," Mandy snaps at the two of them.

The driver shrugs, clearing her throat and adjusting the mirrors as they begin their descent to The Mainland. However, her second—a tiny woman comically dressed head to toe in camo—continues to stare, not allowing Mandy's outburst to scare her off.

"Seriously, Tam," Mandy says to this relentless stare. "I'm focused. This mission was my idea in the first place," Mandy ends with less annoyance and more conviction in her voice than expected. Tam smiles and places a hand on Mandy's knee.

"And now it's our idea. Our mission," Tam replies giving

her knee a few quick pats. "A mission we plan to succeed at as fast as possible," she finishes and turns back around, leaving Mandy to her thoughts.

Mandy's gaze quickly finds a window and she immediately returns to her chanting. Once again there's no sound, just the motion of her lips. Her left hand stays in her pocket to hold onto her phone, which she knows holds multiple pictures of her son. Unable to bring herself to look at them, she finds some sense of serenity just knowing he's in there. His smiling face, there when she needs him.

54

Having given up on tally marks, Peter's only means of tracking the passage of time now is watching his waste bucket fill and fill, assumedly day after day, until it overflows. Around the two-week mark he's forced to sacrifice one of the room's precious corners as an alternative. Just as he becomes accustomed to the stench, the team of three arrives to empty his bucket and give him scraps of food, and the cycle begins again.

Tian has never used this type of testing or torture before, typically going the starvation route. This demonstrates to Peter that this imprisonment is less about his immortality and more about Tian flexing control. Appreciating the need to get out of this cell before Tian ups the ante, Peter is on his feet the moment light spills through his barred-up window. He's prepared to get answers from the guards by any means necessary. He'll make a mess, if needed. The door opens slowly, and instead of the usual three, Peter sees just one—The Starer.

Taken aback by this turn of events, Peter is speechless. He loses all momentum for the onslaught of questions he had planned. However, Peter is more than ready for some alone time and quickly changes tactics. He'll need to persuade The Starer to join his side. But before Peter can begin any kind of manipulation, a booming voice erupts from the guard.

"Come with me," the man enounces with a voice so deep Peter feels it thunder through the room. He holds the door open. Peter obliges without hesitation and steps out of the cell, unsure of their next move but happy to be out of his tiny chamber. The Starer leads him down the hall just a few doors away and into an identical, albeit cleaner, cell. With some disappointment, Peter enters the new cell followed by the large man. While it has an actual toilet and a cot—*Two significant upgrades*, Peter thinks—it is still a prison.

After a moment, however, he notices the most important aspect of this room. Not an addition, but something missing—the cameras. The two make eye contact with each other and The Starer nods, setting down a tray of grey clumpy mass the other guards refer to as *food*. Peter laughs at this action, having not noticed until this very moment that the guard was even carrying a tray. The Starer gives no reaction. He simply turns and exits, closing the new cell door behind him.

A slew of questions flood Peter as he scarfs down the plate of mush, allowing his brain to take in all that just happened while his body gets as much nourishment as it can out of the disappointing meal before him. So much made so little sense to Peter, and he has no idea what is coming next. Why would this guard risk being seen on camera in the old cell just to take him to a new one? Is this another one of Tian's strange games?

Exhaustion sets in as his body begins to digest his first meal in weeks. Peter lies down on the cot, happy to have this little comfort, and falls asleep immediately, allowing his paranoia to accompany him into his dreams.

55

Landing at The Facility's Air City headquarters, Tian realizes just how long it's been since he's even been off The Mainland. The headquarters are located dead center in a high-rise in the industrial section. Having a fair number of wealthy individuals backing their cause, they are able to take up an entire floor of the building.

Tian finds Jeff, his principal contact, waiting for him as he departs the Air Car. The two men walk from the landing garage to the building while Jeff informs Tian that the child's location has still not been identified. Already aware of this troubling bit of information, Tian accepts the news with the surprise and dismay expected of him, choosing anger as his reactionary emotion.

Tian pretends to not understand how they can somehow know the existence of the child without having any idea where the infant is now. He restrains himself from going full-blown asshole, sprinkling in a few curses and insults for good measure. Picking up his pace, Jeff replies to Tian's anticipated response.

"I realize this is incredibly disappointing, sir. As you know, we had a spy at the initial Air Colony Mandy gave birth on, but since then they have moved the child around to a new location on a nearly a daily basis. The Near Mortals use other babies as decoys, and honestly," Jeff continues in a lower tone, "we can't keep up with them. It seems they know we're coming and are staying well ahead of us."

Tian already knows all this, but he's still disappointed in the lack of determination this young man demonstrates. Tian decides to continue playing his *enraged boss* role.

"Well, Jeff, I suppose you need to gather your team and get ahead of them then," Tian responds with less rage and more displeasure in his voice.

"Yes, sir," Jeff whimpers and they continue the rest of their walk and elevator ride in silence. As they reach Tian's temporary office space, Jeff unlocks the door and turns to leave Tian to his business. However, Tian decides he wants to ensure this gentleman understands the urgency of his mission.

"And Jeff," Tian calls out, causing Jeff to turn around. "I will need this alternative plan by day's end." A panicked look appears on Jeff's face. He opens his mouth to reply, but Tian cuts him off. "No excuses, Jeff. Today by six," Tian states simply and then enters his office, promptly shutting the door behind him.

As he settles in, Tian notes that this office space is nearly identical to his upstairs office at The Facility. It has slightly less square footage, but the downgraded technology is all the same. Ready to get down to business, Tian unrolls the only piece of decor he needs to make himself feel right at home—his poster of the solitary hand reaching out of the darkness. He quickly hangs it across from his desk with a couple of pushpins, wanting to reflect on it often. As an added bonus, it will be the last thing any of his visitors will see as they exit, allowing the image to linger.

Sitting down at the desk, Tian takes out his trusty notepad and begins scribbling down a new list of items he needs to focus on. He knows Jeff will not be bringing him a plan anywhere near satisfaction by his deadline. Looking up at his poster, Tian takes a moment to be still. He's been in motion since word hit that the child was born, and he realizes even he needs a moment to stop. Reflecting on the fact that he will find the child with absolute confidence and resolve, Tian kicks his feet up on his desk, hunkers down in his chair, and allows himself to relax for a moment. Soon he will attend meeting after meeting, bouncing around from one Air Colony to the next. But in this moment, Tian allows himself to drift off to sleep.

56

Raised in a generation that's main transportation was still very much earthbound, silly as it was, Air Cars still astound Mandy. The ability to move both horizontally and vertically seems like sheer genius as far as she's concerned. No longer mouthing her mantra, thoughts like these distract her as they near the safe house they must make a quick detour at. Her thoughts transition from amazement to maneuverability as she reflects on how crucial vertical mobility will be for the stealth needed on this operation.

Pulling two miniature versions of old-school walkie-talkies out of her pocket, Mandy checks for the fifth time that they are dialed to the right frequency. They've opted for this form of communication over their implants to hide in plain sight. With the walkie-talkie being so easy to tap into, the chance of Tian looking for this kind of signal over other sophisticated systems will be slim in the heat of the moment. Satisfied that they're set up correctly, Mandy places both instruments back in her pocket.

Finally reaching their destination, Mandy squeezes her way out of the back seat, pulling her luggage along with her. Looking up, she sees that Tam is already out and holding the front door of the safe house open for her, the driver already disappearing inside. Speeding up, Mandy enters and is taken aback by the vast interior. From the outside this house appears to be a small cottage, but its secret is that the owners, instead of building up, built down. Walking in, she's stunned by this cavernous structure.

Having already visited the hideout a handful of times,

Tam doesn't so much as pause, heading straight down the staircase to join the others. Mandy follows, amazed at the impressive sight of this architectural feat. She wants to take her time and feel the exposed rock walls but realizes that her attention and time is needed elsewhere. She promises herself that a return trip will happen once her life is set right.

"It's so nice to finally meet you, Mandy," an extremely tall woman with distractingly thick-rimmed glasses says while extending a hand for shaking.

"You as well," Mandy replies after an awkward silence, not recognizing this woman. She returns the handshake as she looks around the room at the team assembled.

"I'm Sara, the host of this house," she continues with a warm smile, gesturing to the large room they currently occupy. Sara leads Mandy over to the large table in the middle of the room and Mandy pulls out the plans from her bag for tomorrow evening's escape. Spreading out multiple sheets of paper, a large map, and the smuggled blueprints, she organizes them into quadrants. Fortunately, the assembled team is already very well versed in the plan, so only a brief overview will be needed.

"I know everyone has all this down pat, so I just want to go over the key points one more time," Mandy says to the group of people standing in a semicircle around her. With no voiced objections, Mandy continues, pointing at various areas of the map as she speaks. "Tam and I will be dropped off in the back and let in by one of my dear friends at The Facility. I received word yesterday that Tian is off campus for the moment, so security will be more lax than normal. This will make it much easier to access all the people we need to."

Mandy pauses to make sure everyone is following. They stare expectantly at her, so she continues.

"From here, the two of us will make our way to the holding cells for the children. All the children will secretly be prepared that morning to leave. Implementing the buddy system, we will then take the children back out the exit we initially snuck in through. Outside they will find a caravan waiting for them above, ready to deploy at the signal from the walkie-talkie. A beautiful cascade of Air Cars will drop down, allowing the children to pile in and be taken to the Air Colony that awaits them."

Mandy takes in a deep breath, leaving this last image floating out for all of them to grab on to. The room buzzes with excitement as small side conversations begin. Tam heads over to Mandy as she gathers up her papers. Nearly done, she overhears a name drifting in and out of these dialogues.

Peter.

Realizing this too needs to be addressed, Mandy loudly clears her throat to gain the attention of the room again.

"I'm hearing a name surface and yes, you are correct. We did lose a valuable asset with during mine and Max's liberation. There are plans set in motion to retrieve Peter as well, but priority number one for the mission is the children." She hates saying such things, longing for Peter to be by her side, but she pushes back her remorseful emotions and forces a strong smile on her face. "Let's not lose focus. Tomorrow's operation will run smoothly, and then we can focus on our second recon mission," Mandy finishes, and all conversation goes back to normal. Mandy shoves the few remaining papers into her bag, Tam reaching for her as she excuses herself from the room. They both head to the nearest hallway. Before Mandy can say anything, Tam leans in.

"Are you alright?" Tam asks gently.

"I will be," Mandy replies with a trembling voice, avoiding direct eye contact. They continue walking down the hall in silence until they find a small room to duck into.

"We will get him out too. You have to know that," Tam says with a look of concern on her face as they both sit on the floor in this vacant room.

"I do know it. And I know he can handle whatever punishment he is currently receiving because of us. I just wish we could have planned it out, to get Peter on our first try as well." Trying not to let her emotions get away from her, Mandy looks away as she feels tears begin to well up. Tam takes a deep breath that only comes with revealing something you're not supposed to.

"Look, Mandy," she begins, touching Mandy's shoulder to regain her attention.

"I know," Mandy sharply says and shrugs off Tam's touch. "The children come first. But the moment they are safe I'm back in there to free Peter."

"Look," Tam continues calmly. "I'm really, really not authorized to tell you, but…" Tam trails off as Mandy turns around to face her, wiping tears off her cheeks. "We have an inside man, and we are currently working on liberating Peter as well." This last part Tam reveals quickly, unsure of the reaction she's about to receive.

Mandy stares blankly for a moment. Unsure what to do with silence, Tam begins to fill it.

"We needed you focused on the children, so we created this addition to the plan without you," she explains.

Mandy remains motionless.

"But we are sure that he will be rejoining us very soon," Tam continues.

Mandy's expression goes through multiple emotions, landing on what Tam had been afraid of—anger.

"So, you're saying…" Mandy begins slowly. "This entire time I've been drowning in guilt about planning an escape that doesn't include the man I love, you and your team, without telling me, have been planning his escape? That you just let me live with this shame for months now?" Mandy spews, absentmindedly clenching and unclenching her fists.

Tam scrambles to find the words to apologize.

Mandy continues to cycle through emotions before her entire body begins to relax and her expression goes blank. Taking a deep breath, Mandy takes Tam's hands into hers, making intense eye contact.

"Thank you," Mandy expresses to Tam.

Tam is filled with a mix of confusion as relief graces her face.

"I would have loved to be a part of the planning, but

you and your team were right. I needed to focus on my task. Of course, I was going to stay down here and get him out on my own, but now I can move forward less distracted knowing you've got Peter taken care of." Mandy releases her friend's hands and gives her a long, tight hug. Tam finds tears forming in her own eyes now.

Picking up her bag, Mandy begins to get up.

"Hey," Tam states, blinking the tears away. "Not to bring up even more emotions here, but I had no idea you knew that Tian is already on the move." Mandy sits back down, knowing that this conversation would be happening as well.

"I trust our team, Tam. I know that with Tian actively looking for Max that he's in more peril than normal, but as you know, we have contingency plan on top of contingency plan to keep his location secret. I know you are thinking this is an enormous distraction, but until literally a minute ago, Peter was too. So really, I'm less distracted now than I was when I first started our descent down here this morning," Mandy replies, hoping this will be the end of it.

"If you're sure," Tam says with a raised eyebrow.

Mandy stands, ready to grab some alone time before tomorrow's operation.

Tam gestures with her arm towards the open doorway. Mandy takes this as a go-ahead and leaves, heading directly to the room she had been given direction to in an email a few days prior to departure. At the time she had found this amusing, but now she's grateful to have a map and a room to herself for the evening.

57

Near Mortals.

Near Corpses.

He looks over this accomplishment, swelling with pride. A sea of bodies lying deep underground. The last of this sickness locked away.

Nearly through the exit, a movement catches his eye. Unsure why, he's compelled to return. Something is wrong. There is a real person in there. He can feel it.

Tian wades through the unmoving bodies, making his way towards a single swaying hand. As he reaches it, the hand disappears into the mass of bodies before reappearing a few feet to his right. He redirects, grabs for it, and again it moves.

"Stay still!" Tian shouts. "Don't you know I'm trying to save you?"

The room begins to shake and there's a tremendous boom. Tian looks around and sees two more hands pop up near the original, followed by two more booms.

The booms turn into a succession of knocking.

Tian jerks up from his sleeping position.

"Yes? Come in," he blurts out as he tries to rapidly shake off his sleep. In walks the second-in-command assigned to him while he jumps between Air Colonies, a troubled look drawn on his face.

"Yes?" Tian snaps in response to this worrisome look, which immediately disappears from his second's face.

"Sorry, sir. There were just some strange noises coming from your office, and then it took a while for you to respond to my knocking."

"And you came to my office because?" Tian demands, avoiding any further conversation surrounding his dreams with a subordinate.

"You requested an update by 3 p.m., sir," he responds, looking down at the antique wristwatch he's never without. It's one of this second's best qualities as far as Tian is concerned. "It's a few minutes past," he quietly gets out.

"Well?" Tian asks, feeling the last bit of his dream fall away and his impatience rapidly creeping in. His second startles and looks back up from his watch.

"Sir?" his second stammers.

"I'm pretty sure it wasn't an update on the time I wanted," Tian expresses, finding his patience waning.

"Right. The boy, sir," the second manages to get out. Tian leans forward in anticipation. "There is no new news," he quickly says, now nervously winding his watch. Tian falls back in his seat.

"So, you came back here to tell me nothing?" Tian clarifies.

"Well, I came to check in with you at 3 p.m., sir. As requested," he says with a plain look on his face.

Seeing he is getting nowhere, Tian changes tactics.

"Alright, since there is still no underground information about the boy's location, I'd say it's time we move on from this colony to the next Air Port and see if there's more information there."

"Then I'll have everything packed up and ready by..." his second-in-command trails off, staring expectantly at Tian.

"By morning will be fine," Tian finishes for him.

"Then 8 a.m. it is," he says, once again looking at his watch as if to confirm that 8 a.m. exists on his timepiece before he abruptly turns and leaves.

58

As far as Peter's concerned, the night of his escape attempt starts out a little too similar to that of his and Mandy's escape from the apartment cell. As he's let out by one guard and then transferred to another almost immediately, he recalls the way his last attempt ended. So after the third handoff, Peter thanks and dismisses his unknown handler.

"I truly appreciate what you're trying to do for me, but I've got it from here," Peter whispers to the guard. "Please send my regards along to the rest. If you can instead help by keeping those not on my side distracted, that's all I need."

With a silent nod, the most recent escort retreats. Finally alone, Peter finds himself at the very end of this dungeonesque area, relieved that it dumps him out at the very part of The Facility he knows best. Equipped with the knowledge that Tian is off bouncing between Air Colonies—the main reason his guard friend, the Starer, chose now to help him escape—Peter figures he should be out within the hour, so long as he keeps to his usual route.

Walking as quietly as possible, Peter makes it to the narrow stairwell that goes to the main sublevel, the only way out of this pit. Heart pounding, he sprints up the stairs and opens the hidden panel door a crack. Listening first, he hears nothing. Peeking in, he allows his eyes to adjust to the nearly pitch-black surroundings. After a moment, he also senses no one. True to his silent nod, Peter realizes the last guard Peter interacted with must be doing a great job at distracting the others. He hugs the wall as tightly as possible, inching towards the next stairwell. Finally arriving, he's about to make a dash when he hears a sound in the distance. Freezing in his tracks, he prepares to make a dash to get on the other side of the door when he hears the sound again.

A voice.

A voice he recognizes.

59

The first vehicle drops Mandy and Tam off a couple blocks behind The Facility before heading straight up to join the rest of the caravan. The back gate slides open as they dash towards it, allowing them both to slip in. From there, a pair of male guards let them in through a camouflaged exit in the building's rear.

"Thank you," Mandy whispers to the larger of the two men, noting his statuesque appearance and the odd placement of a quirky smile that appears on his face.

Once in, they head down a narrow, winding staircase that drops them off near the back of the warehouse. Thanks to her firsthand knowledge and having studied the maps and blueprints for months, Mandy's able to lead Tam straight to the orphanage. Opening the door, a cold shiver goes up Tam's spine at the sight of all these little children sitting quietly on their bunks. In unison, they all turn their heads at once to see who's entering. Mandy cuts in front of Tam and goes to the slender woman with straight black hair standing near the entrance.

"I'm assuming they're all ready?" Mandy questions.

"Yes," the woman replies in a low voice. "I told them they are going on a long field trip," the woman says, lowering her voice even more so only Mandy can hear her. "Please keep in mind, most of the girls have been raised here. They know nothing of the outside world. It will take some time for them to adjust."

Mandy is aware of this heartbreaking fact. But knowing and facing would be two vastly different things. Nodding at this information, she looks out at the rows of cots and children staring back at her. Each one of these healthy but pale faces looks expectantly towards Mandy. They are all equipped with small suitcases beside them, a mix of excitement, confusion, and hesitation floating in the air.

"And you're sure you can't come with us?" Mandy asks the woman.

"I need to ensure you get out of here with them all. I've actually stayed too long already. Once the coast is clear, I will meet up with you all," she says to Mandy. With a handshake and a nod in Tam's direction, she turns and exits.

The level of concern rises as the children are left with two new adults. Mandy looks back out to the children and gives them a warm smile.

"Raise your hand if you're ready for the field trip," she playfully whispers with as much enthusiasm as the best children's entertainer could deliver.

All but two immediately raise their hands.

"Perfect," Mandy says with a light clap while Tam goes over to the two who seem hesitant and has a little chat. Mandy continues, "I'm Mandy and this is Tam." Tam looks up and waves with a welcoming smile of her own. "We will be your supervisors today," she finishes and glances over to Tam, who now has the two most apprehensive children in hand.

"Alright," Mandy cheers, clapping her hands together again. "Let's get this show on the road!" They all just stare at her. "That means let's go. Everyone, stand up." They all stand in unison, which sends a slight shiver down Mandy's spine. "Take the hand of your assigned partner." They each reach across the aisle and take a hand. Tam helps her two grab on to one another as she picks up the sleeping baby, no more than nine months old. "Perfect. Now grab your bag and follow Tam out the door."

Tam goes to the front of the room and glances back to make sure they are all falling into line. Not only are they lined up, but they are perfectly spaced. It is obvious that these children have spent a lot of time being moved around in groups.

"Time to play the Quick and Quiet Game," Tam says to the group of onlooking kids. "Keep hold of your buddy no matter what, and the last one to make a sound will get a big prize once we arrive at our destination." All the children, although not terribly talkative to begin with, clench their mouths shut, eyes glistening at the mention of a prize.

"Very good," Mandy says from the back of the room. "Time to head out for the field trip." None of the girls say a word, but the excitement is felt in the room as they exit two by two, for the first time not heading to participate in any kind of testing.

Once the last girl is through the door, Mandy takes one last look around to make sure there isn't anything left behind that could be important to one of these little ladies. Seeing nothing but tidy little beds, she turns to catch up with the group. She can barely make them out in the dark warehouse, their silhouettes only illuminated by random exit signs.

To ensure what she is seeing is indeed her group, Mandy sounds off a quick, "Coo, coo," what is immediately returned by Tam.

Mandy begins lightly running to catch up and is almost upon them when something to her left catches her attention. She slows down and starts off in a different direction, hoping that if it's someone not on their side that she can distract them long enough for the children to escape—sacrificing herself if she must.

After a few moments of not hearing or seeing anyone, she begins to think it's just her nerves. With a few more turns, she is confident it's just that and begins to head back towards the back exit. Jogging towards them, she still feels that something is off. It's all been a little too easy, even having planned the escape to coincide with Tian being off campus. Halting, she holds her breath and closes her eyes, focusing on any out-of-place sounds. The quickness of this action pays off as she hears footsteps coming to an unexpected stop one aisle over.

Shit, shit, shit! she thinks to herself as she stays still for another moment, knowing she can't lead anyone back to the kids. Calculating the time quickly in her head, she realizes that Tam and the children should be nearly outside by now and boarding the Air Car, nearly off to the hideout. Her best option will be to double back and lead this person around awhile longer. She has to make sure enough time elapses for the entire group to escape and then try to get to the exit herself. She knows this plan will leave her stranded, but if she can make it outside she has plenty of contingency plans to work with.

Dying to continue forward, Mandy instead takes a sharp left, running as light on her feet as she can, hoping to keep this person chasing after her. Pursued, but not close enough to make evasion impossible as soon as she's positive enough time has passed.

60

Aww shit! She's gonna run! Peter thinks as he picks up his pace. He wants to call out to her but is unsure if the wrong people will hear his voice, so he continues his pursuit.

Of course she's going to run, he chides himself. *She thinks you're part of The Facility.* He begins to pick up his pace even more when it dawns on him what Mandy's doing and why she's here. Stopping dead in his tracks, he listens for a moment and hears only Mandy's light tread moving farther from him. Knowing now where she's headed, as he's the one who taught her how to get around, Peter moves away from the sound of Mandy running for a moment. He needs to see for himself if she accomplished the one thing that could make her leave their child's side.

As he nears the door to the *Storage Closet,* his arm hairs stand on end with anticipation. Turning the handle, it gives way immediately despite never being unlocked. Peter peeks in and, sure enough, every well-made bed is empty. A smile graces his face as a sense of urgency rises in him, realizing he needs to find Mandy now before she flees and leaves him to find his own way home.

Peter can just barely pick up the sound of Mandy running. His lack of trailing must have thrown her off as she is now running in a tight loop just a few aisles over from where he is. He knows it's a mistake the moment the thought enters his mind, but he can't help himself and decides to go *catch her* instead of announcing his presence. Primarily because he still doesn't know who could be listening, but also because she's nearby and he knows he can get her quickly. Then they can leave this place behind for good.

61

Mandy continues running in a loop. She has no idea where the guard, or whoever it is down here with her, has gone. But even without hearing them for a few moments, she knows they are still here. Positive that enough time has passed, Mandy now needs to locate this person before she can tell which way to escape.

The thought of finding Peter crosses her mind, already having missed her initial ride. Had Tam not told her about the plans already in place to save him, she would be running straight to him. But she knows this is a *one goal accomplished* mission, and the last thing she would want to do is put a hitch in the plans already in process for Peter's escape.

Maintaining her pace, thoughts of Peter continue to flood her mind—their first night together, his kindness towards her despite knowing she was one of Tian's spies, the way their relationship blossomed while in captivity. Becoming overwhelmed with emotion, she's about to stop her jogging when a loud *ting* of metal hitting concrete brings her back to the basement.

The noise emanates from her left. Recognizing it as an attempt to distract her instead of an accident, Mandy takes a deep breath and sprints towards the sound. She hopes this play will be the right one. If it is, her pursuer will again be on her tail, and she'll finally mislead them so she can get out.

62

Damn it, Mandy, Peter thinks. *You're never supposed to run towards the noise!*

Having thrown the tin cup to send her running in his direction, Peter now has to loop around the other way, arriving just in time to see her turn the corner of the tall shelving units. Impressed by the new skills she's picked up in the last few months, Peter realizes he's going to have to work harder to trick her.

Just as he's about to give in and reveal himself, Mandy slips up by taking a shortcut he'd taught her on their first escape attempt. He knows this one well, recalling that there's a gap in the middle where he can cut her off. Peter lightly jogs down it and waits for her.

Hearing her approach, he realizes he has no idea how to surprise her nicely. Not wanting to hurt her or have her hurt him, he begins to rethink this entire idea. With Mandy fast approaching, Peter steps back into the recess of the shelving unit, working through this plan. Too dark to make him out, Mandy runs directly past him and as she does, Peter reaches out to grab her.

63

Running down the hall, she remembers a shortcut. This could be her way out. She only hopes that her pursuer isn't aware that halfway through there's a partially constructed aisle that serves no purpose other than to hide the path to the back exit. This is where she needs to go. The unknown person poorly following her is once again nowhere to be seen or heard. Unwilling to do another twenty laps in one place, she knows it is now or never.

Looking around to make sure she isn't missing anything obvious, Mandy makes a dash for the exit and runs faster than she ever has before. This would have been great for her if she could continue forward with no obstacles. Not so great when an arm comes out of nowhere and clotheslines her.

The wind is immediately knocked out of her as she falls on her back. The feeling of death weighs upon her chest. Her assailant leans over her, but she can't make out what they are saying over the ringing in her ears. Noting that they don't touch or attempt to move her, Mandy blinks her eyes a few times, trying to make out the person above her and works on piecing together why she is not already being hauled away. One more blink and he comes into focus and then disappears out of her line of vision as she kicks his legs out from under him.

Wanting to laugh but knowing they need to remain silent, they both sit up and immediately embrace. Mandy shoots a questioning look to Peter and receives one back translating into *I'll tell you later*. Getting back to their feet, Mandy knows Tam will have followed her instructions not to wait on her and the last of the escape vehicles will have departed by now.

Motioning for Peter to follow, Mandy continues towards

the back door she entered through, hoping it is still open for them to leave. Peter follows close behind, reasoning that if she got in that she must have a way out. As they approach this door Peter snickers to himself, having used this exact exit the first time he ever escaped from The Facility. To his knowledge, this door has remained bolted shut ever since.

But again, figuring Mandy had just gotten in, Peter remains silent. Sure enough, she turns the handle on the door and pushes it open. They pause for a moment to make sure they don't hear anyone following them. To both their relief, the distraction promised to Mandy must still be in place as there is still not one guard in sight. Scurrying up the stairs, Mandy cracks open the door leading outside, once again giving pause. Peter holds his breath in anticipation. After a moment they risk it and step outside.

Not realizing the time of day, Peter is slightly disappointed to come upon a night sky as they exit. He'd wanted to feel the sun's warmth on his face again. But, of course, he's filled with much more gratitude to be free of The Facility once again. Briskly walking, almost breaking into a run, the two of them make it a few blocks before they see the entire building light up brighter than either of them have ever seen.

Knowing that the jig is up, they run. Peter continues to follow Mandy as they run as fast as they can for nearly a mile before stopping to catch their breath.

"Where," Peter gets out between gasps of air, "are we headed?"

"A safe house," Mandy whispers. "I've discovered an entire network of allies since last we've been together," she finishes and begins running again with Peter right beside her. Having memorized several ways to get from The Facility to this base, Mandy and Peter are able to get there in less than an hour's time. Both are drained from the constant running but are happy to be somewhere safe for the evening.

"Mandy," a woman Mandy only knows by sight from the night before shouts as they enter the safe house. "Am I glad to see you," this woman continues. "Per your instructions, the entourage of children and the rest of your team headed straight back to the community," she explains, pausing for a moment to choke back her emotions. "We thought we lost you, my dear," she continues, now standing even closer. "But here you are." Her gaze moves from Mandy to Peter. "And with Peter no less," she finishes and grasps his hands into her own.

"You both must be bushed," another woman speaks up. The first woman takes the cue and releases Peter's hands, turning to the second woman.

"Of course they are. Goodness, of course you are," she continues, now facing Mandy and Peter again. "We have a room set up for you just down the hall. You can sleep here tonight, and we will get you back up to the community first thing in the morning." Seeing Mandy's anxious expression, she adds, "You don't want to travel tonight, dear. They'll be looking for you everywhere right now. Best to lay your head down, gather your strength, and head home in the morning."

With that, the second woman takes them straight to the prepared room. Collapsing on the bed the moment the door closes, they both turn to look at each other as the realization of just how overjoyed they are to be back together settles in. Exhausted, they merely intertwine and settle into a beautifully long kiss before passing out for the night. Happily reunited.

64

Tian lets out a long sigh. With no way to figure out where the child is, he has zero leverage over Peter or with the other board members. He needs this child in order to unlock the key to the disease once and for all.

With this thought Tian packs up the few items in this tiny office he's been using, mainly his laptop, scraps of notepaper, and his beloved poster, not needing a lot when hopping between The Air City and its countless Air Colonies. With all his belongings in tow, he stands and is ready to go back to his room when there's a knock at his door.

"Yes?" Tian calls out, a tinge of annoyance in his voice. In the doorway is his second-in-command, white as a ghost. Before Tian can dismiss him, he barges into the room.

"They're gone, sir! All of them, gone!" he blurts out.

"Who's gone?" Tian asks as he sets his stuff on the desk in front of him. His second just shakes his head back and forth.

Opening his mouth, "Gone," is all that comes out.

"Fuck!" Tian blurts out, slamming his hand on the desk. "Peter's escaped *again*?"

"More," he replies, avoiding eye contact.

"More? Damn it, what's going on?" Tian comes around his desk to be face-to-face with his second. "Take a deep breath and tell me now. Who. Is. Gone?" A deep breath is taken, for Tian the longest breath of his life, and then he finally speaks.

"P-P-P-Peter, yes. But also, the ch-ch-children. All the little girls. They are all gone." Tian nearly falls over, catching himself on the edge of his desk, the only thing keeping him standing. Tian's complexion matches that of his second.

"Well, that just can't be," Tian finally says with almost a laugh. "Where did you get this information?" Tian inquires.

"From the main office, sir. They want you to return im-im-immediately," he stammers, fidgeting with his watch now and wishing it could transport him forward in time, free of his boss's ire.

"The main office, huh?" Tian replies with eerie calmness, returning to the other side of his desk. He then begins purposefully rifling through his office supplies. "Needing us back, are they?" Tian asks, pulling out a sheet of fresh paper.

"Yes, sir. I already have both of our rooms packed."

"That's great. You finish making the travel arrangements then," Tian says as calmly as possible. "Return to get me when we are ready to depart."

"Yes, sir," he quickly replies and darts out the door.

Tian begins laughing as he sits down at his desk. He grabs a pencil out of his box to go with the paper and writes *TO-DO LIST* at the top followed by:

FIND BOY
FIND GIRLS
FIND PETER

Taking a deep breath, his laughing stops at the sight of his completed list. Shaking his head, he moves down the sheet of paper to the middle and draws a firm, straight line. Above which he writes:

The main objective stays the same.
FIND BOY

Underneath this he writes:

This will solve EVERYTHING!

Then Tian draws three dark lines underneath.

He meticulously folds this paper in half, then fourths, then eighths. He presses each edge to make sure it's as flat as possible and gingerly places it in the breast pocket of his coat. Taking another deep breath in, he rolls his neck from side to side, allowing it to crack. With his box of office supplies in hand, Tian no longer wishes to wait for his second to return and exits, off to find him. And then the boy.

65

Emerging from their room, Mandy and Peter take a quick shower, feeling more relaxed than either could have expected.

Then entering the main gathering area of the safe house, they are greeted by a handful of faces Mandy recognizes from the day prior.

"Good morning," booms a boisterous woman with a grand smile and an outreached hand. Mandy accepts it first, followed by Peter as she continues. "I'm Sam. I didn't get to properly meet you the other night when all the planning was going down, Mandy. I'm the caretaker of this humble abode," Sam finishes with a mock-curtsy.

"You do an outstanding job," Mandy replies.

"I'd extend an invitation for breakfast, but I know we already have a car ready for you to get back. We received some wonderful news this morning. All the children arrived safely to the Air Colony. As expected, they're all a bit confused by the new surroundings but are being worked with on a one-on-one basis to ensure their quick adjustment to freedom."

Mandy's flooded with relief, followed by a yearning to have her baby in her arms again. They are offered a tote bag full of food from one of the women standing in the great room and Peter takes it, thanking them in the process. Sam motions for them to follow her, and they all head down a hallway leading to the garage.

"Peter, I can't tell you just how happy we all are that you were able to escape as well," Sam comments. "We were a bit worried when you didn't make it out with the others, Mandy. But arriving here with Peter last night was the best outcome any of us could have hoped for," she finishes with a gleeful smile as she opens the door to the garage.

"I'll second that," Peter replies, grabbing Mandy's hand and giving it a squeeze.

"Seeing that we need the car back, Mary is going to drive you back to the hideout," Sam reports and nods to the redhead waiting near a yellow Air Car. The woman immediately reminds Peter of his favorite cabbie, Charlotte, and smiles at the sight of her, while Mandy's face shows more concern. Sam adds off Mandy's expression, "We chose the yellow one on purpose. Hiding in plain sight, you see."

This does nothing to set Mandy at ease, but she knows it's her only option, as this is the only car she sees in the garage. Aching to be home, Mandy extends her hand to receive one more firm handshake from Sam.

"You two go ahead and sit in the back together, I'm sure you have a lot to catch up on and I've got a great podcast I'm dying to get back to," Mary says as she gets into the driver's seat, twice tapping her right temple. They do as they're told and climb into the back of the car, already in flight before either can secure their seatbelts. Exiting the compound, Mandy slides down in her seat, practically sitting on the floor by the time they enter the traffic above.

"Need any help down there?" Peter inquires, looking down at her.

"Funny, Peter," Mandy hisses. "You should join me. Tian is still out and about. The last thing we need is to let our guard down when we're so close to being done." Peter extends his hand and pulls Mandy back up in the seat.

"The last thing we need is to get in an accident and have you flying out of your seatbelt."

"I appreciate that, but no. I'm staying down here," Mandy replies as she quickly ducks back down.

"Okay, well I'm going to stay up here, but I'll make sure I turn my face towards you," he says leaning forward a bit. "I'm fortunate enough to have a very nondescript back of the head, so we should be good there."

More than a little annoyed, Mandy says nothing, just wanting to be back with Max.

66

Crawling into the backseat of his second's Air Car, Tian closes the door behind him and slumps down in his seat. The thought of the upcoming conversation he will have with the rest of the board once he's back on The Mainland makes his stomach do flips. The only thing calming him down is his list. Each time he thinks about it he desperately places his hand over his right breast pocket, needing this sense of order to maintain his composure for the duration of this ride.

Even with the situation as it currently is, he knows he can find the boy. The rest of the children—and even Peter to a lesser degree—are all mere pawns, things to play with. But this child is his key, the tool to unlock the true cause of the disease and the way to finally eradicate it. He knows once he has the boy in his possession that he can bring the board back to his side.

This thought brings a slight smile to Tian's face, as he has full confidence in himself, the one person who has never let him down. Glancing out the window at the cars passing by, he for once finds himself appreciating this view and the nondescript faces flying past. Not paying attention to any one individual, Tian enjoys the flow of them passing by, falling into sync with them. Feeling almost calm, he's about to drift off when the motion of a woman's head popping into sight causes him to focus. After a moment of taking in the contents of this car, Tian gasps and quickly ducks down.

"Dumb fucking luck!" are the first words that escape Tian's gaping mouth, urgently followed by, "I don't care how you do it, but you must follow the yellow car that's across from us." He emphasizes, "You *cannot* lose this car!"

"Yes, sir," his second replies and flips the blinker on, preparing to merge over to the turn lane. As the light goes from red to green, they pull a U-turn in front of the car in question and drive slowly, allowing the yellow vehicle to catch up and then pass them. Tian remains crouched on the floor in the back the entire time.

Confused about what's going on, his second opens his mouth to inquire but stops as the yellow car passes them and he sees the head of Mandy duck out of sight to create a clear shot of Peter's mug.

"Dumb fucking luck indeed!" his second echoes with disbelief.

His temporary second proves to be a great tail. They're able to follow the two all the way back to a smaller outlying community they assume is their hideout. Impressed with his second's ability to keep distance without losing their target, Tian contemplates for a moment telling him such but then thinks better of it. He needs this man to maintain focus, finding that too much praise can only weaken a subordinate.

As the yellow Air Car begins its descent to the outlying community, his second circles back just in time to see which corner of this small Air Colony they're headed towards. Not seeing much traffic, they decide to wait until nightfall to make their actual approach and park their vehicle on the outskirts of this small floating structure.

Giddier than he's been in years, Tian sits in silence as he waits for the sun to set, not wanting to jinx all their good luck by talking. His second happily takes this time to catch up on sleep, reclining his chair and placing one arm over his eyes to block out the setting sun. Tian stays alert and removes the paper from his pocket. Reading it over, he is ready to cross the top objective off his list.

67

There have been many important and extraordinary moments in Peter's life up to this point, yet all pale in comparison to meeting his son. He watches from afar as Mandy rushes to Max, taking the reaching child from Fran's arms. Mandy swoops up her young one, the mother and child giggling together as they glide towards Peter. Still unaware that he should be afraid of strangers, the child immediately reaches out to Peter, who accepts him with open arms and pulls him close to his chest. After a moment of snuggling, the child squirms, preferring to face out towards the open world than to be held close, at least when he is so alert. Unsure of what to do, Peter holds him at arm's length, straight out from his body.

"Here," Mandy gently says with a smile as she adjusts Peter's arms, one to cradle the bottom and the other to wrap around the small torso, allowing the child to lean back on Peter's chest. As this tender moment comes to an end, Peter and Mandy look up and become aware that there are several people gathered in this small room. They notice that most of them are young girls between the age of five and thirteen, with one infant just older than Max.

"I seriously can't believe our luck here, Peter," Mandy comments. "Everything just seems like it went too smoothly."

"Maybe on your end," Peter replies with a slight smile.

"You make a good point," Mandy responds as she looks over and sees Tam motioning for her to come over.

Leaving the baby with Peter, Mandy goes over and sees the children's straight-haired caretaker who helped them escape. A wave of relief and joy fills her. They really did do it. They saved all the children and reunited her little family. Now all that's left is to distribute these children among the underground movement. There are plenty of women that would love a family of their own. Then she can take her family and get as far away from The Facility as the Air Colonies will allow.

After glancing back at Peter, who's completely enveloped in doting on their child, she turns to Tam and heads out to the small back office where they can complete all these plans. In just a few short days, the children will have proper homes, and she will be free to live her new life.

68

The beautiful thing about these smaller Air Colonies is the ease in which you can get in and out of them, Tian thinks to himself as the sun dips into the horizon. Most, like this one, only consist of a handful of buildings. These floating structures were originally built as storage areas alongside The Air City during construction. Once the project ended, they were left to the wayside and commandeered by groups like Mandy's little bunch as hideouts.

Having done his due diligence by studying the layout of each of these leftover scaffoldings, Tian is very familiar with the potential layout of Mandy and Peter's hideaway. They'll be on high alert, of course. Afterall, the only reason the pair pulled off their escape is because he was off campus. There is no expectation of just strolling in and walking right back out with the kid. He'll need to be on point, distraction in hand. That's where his second will come into play.

With one arm draped over his face, sleep is not what Tian's second is currently achieving. Following Mandy and Peter to this outlying air structure can only mean one thing—they are going to retrieve each and every one of the escapees. While he trusts Tian about as far as he can throw him, after weighing out all his options he concludes that waiting until they know exactly what they have here is the best course of action. The last thing he wants is to alert The Facility immediately and end up empty-handed, not wanting to dig the hole he now finds himself in any deeper. If they return without some kind of bargaining chip, as Tian puts it, they might as well find their own hideout and disappear.

Knowing that Tian will wake him when it is time to move,

he lets these thoughts run around his head, ready to confirm this location and get backup as soon as they can.

As the last bit of light disappears over the horizon, Tian knows they still have a few more hours before they can act. Tilting his head back, he closes his eyes and allows himself to daydream about this victory, even if he can't say it out loud yet.

69

Entering their room, Peter sees Mandy fervently writing at a desk, not looking up as he approaches. When he rests a hand on her shoulder, her body melts against his touch, gently leaning into his hand. But she continues to scratch her pen across the page.

"We won," he asserts, placing his other hand on her other shoulder. "It's time to rest." Writing one last sentence, she sets her pen down and turns to him.

"I like where your head is at, but I'm not sure either is entirely true. The Facility still exists. *Tian* still exists. I know I can't put an end to his entire organization, but I sure as hell can try to put an end to *him*." Closing her notebook, she gets up from her chair and crosses the room to change into her nightwear. Frustrated and ready to leave the past in the past, Peter follows her.

"Mandy," he begins. "You can't keep going like this. You went back and saved all those girls, and accidentally me," he says with a smile and walks over to her. "It's time we start anew. You, me, and Max. We can be a family," Peter pleads.

"I do want to be a family with you, Peter. But how can you ask me to just turn away from this atrocity? If you know anything about me, you should know that I can't just turn away and let this evil organization continue to exist. And please don't forget that Tian is still out there. He could be on his way to recapturing us all right now."

They cross to the foot of the bed and sit down.

"We have guards on the lookout right now, Mandy," Peter responds, placing his arms around her. "I know Tian is sneaky and that he has a vast network."

Mandy shoots him a *this is not helping* look.

"*But* we also have connections, a network we didn't even know we were a part of until recently." Peter pauses to think of his next move. "Okay," he continues. "What if we find our safe place, and then *we* begin our next move against Tian and everything he's aligned with?"

Mandy takes a moment, pretending to think on this, and then leans over and gives Peter a passionate kiss.

"That sounds perfect," she sighs, trying to be quiet with Max slumbering in their room.

"I know we met in a very strange and forced way, but I love you, Mandy. I've never known anyone like you, and I've known a lot of people," Peter says, looking deeply into Mandy's eyes.

Blushing, Mandy smiles at this.

"I've also been caught many times by Tian before, but I've never felt as helpless as I did this time. I never had someone to sincerely miss. This made me realize that I want to continue sharing my life with you," Peter continues as he transitions from the bed to bending on one knee in front of her. He then takes her left hand and ties a ribbon around her ring finger. No words need to be exchanged as Mandy takes Peter's face in her hands and begins kissing him.

They both fall back on the bed, Peter holding Mandy as she looks at the most romantic piece of cloth she's ever seen. She realizes that Peter is right. Yes, Tian's currently on the move, but he will always be *on the move.* The only way to truly win is to let Tian go and to live her life. She is finally ready and able to do just that.

70

The entire community hovers in the kind of silence that comes after a night of celebration. Having given adequate time for everyone to let their guard down for the evening, Tian shakes his second, annoyed he's been asleep this entire time. Trying to seem like he's just awoken from a deep sleep, the second jolts up, eyes blinking.

"Everything seems nice and still," Tian says to his second. "You leave the car running and I'll go scope out the location." They both open their car doors simultaneously, causing Tian to shoot back a look at his second.

"You said to leave the car running, which I am," he says off Tian's leering, motioning to the ignition. "But as your second-in-command our futures are tied, so I am going with you."

Sensing an argument will only waste valuable time, Tian gives in and nods his head. They both shut their doors as quietly as possible, meeting at the back of the car. Tian hands his second a bottle and a cloth.

"Chloroform," Tian whispers. "Killing anyone right now could draw too much attention," he explains, clutching his own bottle and cloth.

Horrified at this logic, the second follows closely behind Tian, wanting more than ever to be free of this man. Knowing exactly where the happy couple would be shacked up, Tian moves quickly from shadow to shadow, pausing only to ensure no one is around before moving on. His second stays one shadow behind and keeps an eye on their rear. As they near the center of the community, they see two people on lookout with their backs to each other, confirming to Tian that the building they are headed to is indeed where the targets are. Signaling to his second, they both dash at the two women on guard, taking them by surprise and setting them gently on the ground after they've consumed enough of the toxic gas.

"You really do need to stay *right here*," Tian commands. With no further argument, his second nods and turns his back to the entrance to act as a lookout, ready to call The Facility the moment they return to the car with intel.

Tian slowly enters the main courtyard, keeping his back to the exterior wall until he's able to slip into the building. He finds himself in a large room covered wall to wall in sleeping children. He immediately recognizes his entire collection. For a moment he stops, realizing he can easily contact The Facility and recapture them right now. But for Tian, this is not the goal.

He needs *the child*. The only one that matters.

He continues around the exterior of the room, managing to be silent enough to not disturb any of the slumbering children. He finds his way to the rear exit and then into a small makeshift bedroom, and just as he expected, finds the peaceful family unit. Peter, Mandy, and the golden child.

Peeking around the corner, he sees Mandy placing the child into a small bassinet next to the bed. He had figured that if anyone would be in his way, it would be the mother. Waiting to see what she does next, Tian leans against the exterior wall in the hallway, listening intently for some sign of her approach. After a few moments of silence, he peers in again and sees that Mandy has lain back down, now intertwined with Peter in bed with their child sleeping soundly next to them.

He lies in wait nearly twenty minutes until he's sure that both Mandy and the child have fallen back asleep. Holding his breath, Tian then enters the room and makes his way to the side of their bed. Staring at the two of them sleeping, he is distracted by the uncontrollable rage he has for Peter, and now Mandy. Tempted to throw his plan out the window and end at least one of them here and now, he is snapped out of this instinct by the baby stirring. Swiftly and quietly, he approaches the crib and in one fluid motion lifts the still sleeping baby up and holds him to his chest, cradling him in such a way as to not wake him.

Moving through the home, he exits out the opposite of the way he entered, finding himself outside in just a few right turns. From there he's practically running, taking a different path back to the car to ensure he's not seen by his second. Tian wants to leave something for Mandy and Peter to deal with when they awake.

Tian lays the baby down in the back seat, wrapping his jacket around the sleeping child to create a nest of sorts and then using a seat buckle to secure him until he can pick up a car seat. Putting the car in neutral, he allows the momentum of the gravitational pull to silently take the vehicle down halfway to the surface before he starts the car and begins his drive back to The Facility, ready to present his prize.

Glancing in the rearview mirror, he sees the sleeping infant and thinks of the horror his parents will soon be waking up to. The thought brings a smile to his face, knowing that he's won and that he has the child he's worked so hard to obtain. But the idea of just handing him over to his superiors feels wrong. What will they do but run tests on this small human, trying to determine the gene sequence that created this disease in the first place? While Tian wants this plague to be gone as much if not more than anyone, he knows that there is so much more that this child can be used for than a science project. Where will this leave him? The board already made it clear that their patience is running thin on his passion project as it is. Would bringing this baby back to them be the final nail in his own coffin?

As these thoughts begin to multiply, Tian starts searching for a new answer. As brains do when you least expect them to, a memory of a previous conversation Tian had with Peter pops up —the comment about raising this child as his own. Touching his breast pocket, this thought slowly becomes his new goal.

Nearing land, Tian pulls the car up and heads towards the closest Air Colony he can find.

Keeping the child.

That is the answer.

What better way to get back at your enemies than to raise one of theirs to think like yourself? Knowing this car has a tracking device, he realizes he will need to dump it immediately. He can then use his deep web of underground contacts to disappear both himself and *his child*.

As the sun rises, Tian pulls his car to the side of a neighboring Air Colony. He removes the child from the back seat and places the car in neutral, allowing it to eventually fall into the waters below. This will buy him just enough time to get lost in his web and to begin the training of his small Immortal.

Thank you so very much for going on this adventure with me, Near Mortal. I promise the second volume is on its way!

In the meantime, if you enjoyed reading Near Mortal, please don't forget to leave me a review and share it with your nearest and dearest! While you're there, you can follow me on Amazon, Goodreads, Facebook, BookPub, Booksprouts... pretty much wherever you LOVE to follow authors, to keep up-to-date with my subsequent publications.

Be sure to visit my website - www.altyart.com - and sign up for my newsletter. This newsletter will only be sent out when there are updates on publications or other art in the works, so you will never feel like I'm spamming you. The updates will include exclusive release deals and other exciting news from Story Quarry.

Again, thank you for making it this far in my very first novel and I look forward to sharing many more stories with you in the future.

JuliA